YELLOWCAKE
CONSPIRACY

THE
YELLOWCAKE
CONSPIRACY

STEPHEN DAVIES

Andersen Press • London

First published in 2007 by Andersen Press Limited,
20 Vauxhall Bridge Road, London SW1V 2SA
www.andersenpress.co.uk

British Library Cataloguing in Publication Data available

ISBN 978 1 84270 674 9

Typeset by Nigel Hazle
Printed in the UK by CPI Bookmarque, Croydon, CR0 4TD

Acknowledgements

What follows is fiction but it is grounded in reality. I would like to thank the following people for their freely given expertise: David and Nikki Sudlow, Dr Reuben Rubio II, Chuck Manning, Andy James, Nick Harrison, Peter Jones, Jocelyn Elliott, Simon Cross and Keith Smith.

Thanks also to Anout ag Ahmed for his hospitality in Niger, and to editor Rona Selby for her good advice during the writing of this book.

For Charlie

1

'The production of nuclear weapons is on the rise,' said the man on the platform, flinging his hands high into the air to emphasise his statement. 'If we sit by and do nothing it will continue to rise.'

A murmur of agreement, or perhaps of fear, ran round the conference hall. In the front row, Dr Talata knit his brows and sighed. The International Atomic Energy Agency's annual meetings in Vienna were never a bundle of laughs, but this one was turning out gloomier than most.

'What is more,' continued Dr Belem, 'the threat of nuclear terrorism hangs over the world like the sword of Damocles.'

Dr Talata glanced sideways at his wide-eyed neighbours. Whoever Damocles might be, the words nuclear and terrorism had evidently hit the mark.

Dr Belem took the microphone off its stand and walked to the front of the platform. 'All of us in the International Atomic Energy Agency are terrified about the possibility that one day an explosive device will be created using . . .' He paused and his voice sank to a confidential whisper '. . . *stolen nuclear material.*'

The phone in Dr Talata's lapel pocket vibrated silently against his chest. He took it out and looked at it.

READ MESSAGE?
OK

The text message was in his mother tongue, French:

TU CONNAIS SILVA?

Dr Talata bridled. Did he know SILVA? What *didn't* he know about SILVA? He stabbed out a reply:

WHO R U?
SEND

On the platform, Dr Abdul Belem had put his microphone back on its stand and was reading from his notes: 'The IAEA must be vigilant. We must work with governments and security services to prevent the theft of nuclear materials . . .'

Dr Talata's phone vibrated in his palm.

> ### READ MESSAGE?
> ### OK
> ### WE R YR NXT EMPLOYR.
> ### WE HV CAKE.
> ### WE NEED IT BAKED.

Talata cocked his head to one side. There was no way to tell if this was a genuine job offer. It could be a trap. His thumbs danced over the keypad of his phone:

> ### WHERE R U?
> ### SEND

'Terrorism is a hydra,' Belem was saying. 'Cut off one head, another grows in its place. Together we must formulate a range of detection and response measures . . .'

> ### READ MESSAGE?
> ### OK
> ### I'M RIGHT BEHIND U.

The hairs on the back of Dr Talata's neck stood on end. *This could be interesting*, he thought.

*

Haroun woke to find that the sun had already risen. He was glad to see the sun and the vast open sky. In his dream he had been down in the mine and the roof of the tunnel had collapsed on either side of him. *Pullo yidaa ombeede*, went the Fulani proverb. *A Fulani man does not like to be enclosed.*

His elder brother Hamma was watching him with a frown of disapproval. 'By the time the first cow got up this morning, I heard her,' he said. 'Even before the first ray of the sun touched her horns, I had already washed my ears and prayed.'

Haroun sat up and rubbed the crick in his neck.

'You are no longer a Fulani,' continued Hamma. 'The cows could all have wandered off and got lost while you were asleep and you would not have heard a thing.'

'I wish *you'd* wandered off and got lost while I was asleep,' said Haroun. He crouched on his haunches next to the water bucket and washed his face and neck.

'And you missed dawn prayer,' said Hamma, shaking his head. 'Look where the sun is. Even if you do your prayers now, it is too late.'

Hamma had been like this ever since Haroun got a job in the Tinzar uranium mine; he was jealous because Haroun was in paid work and he was not. He should be grateful, thought Haroun. After all, it was

4

the mining wage that paid for Hamma's cola nuts.

Haroun prayed, then rolled up his grass sleeping mat and put it in his hut. His brother Hamma began to herd the cows, twirling his staff to make the lazy ones stand up. '*Oss, oss!*' he cried, and the cows moved off towards the pasture in the west. They knew the routine.

Tinzar was right on the edge of the arid Sahara desert, but after the annual rains a few acres of green grass appeared to the west of the town. Haroun's family would graze their cows here until the grass was finished and then move on to pastures new. Such was the life of a nomad.

As they walked, the cows kicked up clouds of dust which drifted away on the warm breeze.

'Seems to me that your legs are tired, brother,' called Hamma. 'You have forgotten how to walk.'

'You know nothing,' said Haroun. 'Yesterday I walked from one o'clock in the afternoon to nine o'clock at night.'

Hamma snorted. 'What you do down in that mine is not walking. When a Fulani man walks he walks in the light under an infinite sky. He holds the staff across the back of his shoulders and walks towards the horizon, and in front of him walk a herd of cows. Scrabbling around at the bottom of a dry well is not walking.'

*

Chessvi♛e.fr members

You are logged in as *Agahan*.

Zabri has come to the table.

Play? **YES** I <u>NO</u> **YES**

Agahan:	*Salam aleykum.*
Zabri:	*Aleykum asalam.*
Agahan:	**Fifty years ago, what did the imajaghan desire?**
Zabri:	A fast white dromedary, a red saddle, his sword and a song of love.
Agahan:	**And today, what does the imajaghan desire?**
Zabri:	A plate of rice, a blanket to cover himself, his sword as a souvenir. These security questions bore me.
Agahan:	**They are important. Are you still in Vienna?**
Zabri:	Yes.
Agahan:	**Did you contact Dr Talata?**
Zabri:	Yes. He says he knows SILVA.
Agahan:	**What does he want in return?**
Zabri:	Poetry.
Agahan:	**Don't joke.**
Zabri:	I'm not. He wants the Seven Golden Odes from the National Museum of Jeddah.
Agahan:	**Do we have a man in Jeddah?**
Zabri:	No.

6

Agahan: I will send the Gecko – he will like Saudi Arabia. Salam aleykum.

Zabri: Aleykum asalam.

Agahan has left the table. Play again? <u>YES</u> I <u>**NO**</u> **NO**

*

It was Haroun who first noticed that one of the cows was missing. They had taken the animals in amongst the *chilluki* trees where the grass was tall and lush, and somehow Naaye, his mother's reddish milk-cow, had wandered off.

'I'll go and look for her,' said Hamma. 'You stay here and try not to lose any more of them.'

Haroun waited until Hamma had disappeared into the trees and then he wandered over to a nearby breadfruit tree. He spied a ripe breadfruit high up in the branches, took aim and swung his staff.

'*Salam aleykum*,' said a voice behind him.

Haroun jumped at the sound and his staff flew off into the bushes. A white man was leaning against the *chilluki* tree behind him.

'*Aleykum asalam*,' he said, wondering what a *tuubaaku* was doing here.

'My name is Remy,' said the *tuubaaku*. 'I work for *Bibliothèque Nomadique*.'

Haroun said nothing. He had heard talk of this Frenchman, who had appeared in Tinzar during the last week. They said he had a van full of books which he took from school to school.

'And you must be Haroun,' continued Remy.

'You are the man who walks a hundred miles every week.'

Haroun retrieved his staff from the bushes. He could sense the white man walking alongside him. What could this *tuubaaku* want with him?

'Who told you my name?' said Haroun at last.

'One of the Uranico miners. Is it true you have access to every part of the mine?'

'I am the lamplighter,' said Haroun. 'I can go anywhere.'

'Do you enjoy working at Uranico?'

'Yes,' Haroun lied.

'Do they pay you well?'

Haroun looked at him. 'We Fulanis say that it is shameful to ask a lot of questions.'

The cows were moving off again. Haroun followed them and the *tuubaaku* followed Haroun.

'Would you like to work for me?' said the white man.

'No,' said Haroun.

'You are young and discreet and you know the mine. Come and work for me.'

'No.'

'Why not?'

'I do not know you.'

'I am French. I am a librarian. I travel round in my van and lend books to children.'

'I still do not know you.'

They walked on in silence. The only sound to be heard was the chomping of the cows as they tore tufts of grass out of the hard ground.

'Do they never get full?' asked the tuubaaku.

'Not until afternoon,' said Haroun. 'I saw your library parked near the mine last night,' he added.

'You are observant.'

'I am a herder,' said Haroun. 'If I were not observant I would have no cows left.'

Remy gave a sudden yelp and hopped about in pain. He had stood on a *chilluki* thorn, a vicious spike which could pierce even the toughest sandals. Haroun leaned on his staff and watched the white man's antics. *What a shameful display. A grown man should bear pain in silence.*

'This work you want me to do,' said Haroun. 'What kind of work is it?'

'Research,' said Remy, sitting down and taking off his sandal. 'I want you to find out things for me.'

'Things about the mine?'

'Yes. I need you to ask questions.'

Haroun walked away. 'When a man asks questions in Tinzar he loses his job,' he said.

'Haroun, listen to me,' called Remy. 'I believe your mine director Monsieur Gerard is in danger.'

'What?'

'There are bad things going on at your mine.'

Haroun swallowed. 'Go and talk to our director Monsieur Gerard about it,' he said.

'I tried,' said the white man. 'He won't talk to me.'

'Then neither will I.' Haroun broke into a run.

The cows would scatter if he did not round them up quickly.

'Wait!' called Remy. 'There is a red cow tied to the baobab tree over there.'

Haroun's head spun. '*You* took Naaye? You stole my cow?'

'Forgive me,' said Remy. 'I had to talk to you on your own, you see. Borrowing a cow was the only way to split you and your brother up. If you change your mind, come and see me at the library.'

Haroun herded the cows towards the baobab tree that Remy had pointed to. *A Fulani does not feel fear,* he told himself.

*

Aziz waited at the luggage carousel and checked his watch. Five o'clock. It had been a long journey: Algiers to Jeddah, changing planes at Tripoli. Jeddah was close to Mecca and most of his fellow passengers were heading there on the Hajj, the Muslim pilgrimage.

He picked his two cases off the conveyor belt and walked towards customs, sweating. Jeddah airport was not air-conditioned. The temperature this afternoon was about 38 degrees and the gecko suit under his clothes made it feel hotter.

A young, clean-shaven customs officer beckoned him over. 'Open the cases,' he said.

Aziz had two cases: a small black suitcase and a long canvas bag. He opened the first case. Trousers, socks, shirts, gloves, books, night-vision goggles.

The customs officer held up the goggles and raised an eyebrow. 'Explain,' he said.

'They are for fishing at night,' said Aziz quickly. 'Fly fishing.'

The officer opened the canvas bag. Inside was more fishing equipment: a travel rod in an aluminium tube and a pouch of flies. *A Gecko likes his flies.*

'Nice flies,' said the officer, peering into the pouch. 'Did you make them yourself?'

'Yes,' said Aziz. 'Do you think they'll fool the fish?'

The officer looked at the night-vision goggles, and back at the flies. '*Inshallah*,' he said at last. 'If God wills it, your flies will fool the fish. Welcome to the Kingdom of Saudi Arabia. Please do not empty the kingdom of all its marine life.'

Aziz thanked him and walked through the double doors out into the arrivals concourse. He went straight to a cash dispenser and took out a thousand Saudi riyalh. All he needed now was a SIM card for his phone and a hire bike. When the heist was over, he told himself, he would take off this stifling gecko suit and have a long, cool shower.

2

'Fulani! Hey, Fulani!'

Haroun turned round slowly and winced. The light was shining in his eyes and blinding him.

'Fulani! Where are you going?'

It was the shrill voice of Blaise Soda, the foreman, second-in-command at the Tinzar uranium mine. When the light shone away from Haroun's eyes he saw that Soda was accompanied by his pet ferret. The ferret was sitting on the foreman's shoulder and grinning its buck-toothed grin.

'Remind me,' said Haroun. 'Which of you two is the foreman?' He spoke in Fulani, a language Soda did not understand. Insulting Blaise Soda in Fulani always cheered Haroun up.

'Either speak French or look for another job,' said Soda. 'Where you are going?'

'Gallery 28A. There is a burst bulb there.'

'Leave it. We need you at Dynamite Face B. There is a problem.'

Haroun scowled. 'That is not my job,' he said.

This afternoon's shift had been unpleasant enough already without finishing it in a hundred pieces. Attending to problems at the dynamite face usually involved retrieving unexploded dynamite, a dangerous job which should be carried out by a robotic arm.

Soda's shrill voice rose even higher. 'Your job is to obey my instructions!' he cried. 'If I tell you to go to Gallery 28A, you go. If I tell you to come to Dynamite Face B, you come. If I tell you to come to Face B on one leg, you hop. Is that clear, Fulani?'

Haroun turned his trolley around and began to trundle in the direction of the dynamite face. '*Je viens*,' he said. This was Uranico, after all. Why would they spend money on a robotic arm when there was a Fulani arm in the mine?

Blaise Soda plodded off. Somewhere down the tunnel a tannoy crackled.

'*Bonsoir, mes frères*,' came a voice over the tannoy. 'This is your director Claude Gerard speaking. The time is 6 o'clock, the temperature at ground level in Tinzar is 32 degrees. Work hard and work carefully. Make sure you are wearing your helmet and your face mask. Make sure your trousers are tucked into your boots. I am going home soon. Warm greetings to you and your families.'

Haroun smiled. Claude Gerard had never met any of the workers' families, but it was good of him to pass on his greetings.

'*Inan amiiru mon Claude Gerard ina haala. Laasara wari, yaasin na wuli . . .*'

The director loved African languages and he made all his announcements in Fulani, Zerma and Tamasheq, the mother tongues of his employees. It was his way of showing them respect.

Haroun bent down and tucked his trousers into his boots.

'Haroun!'

Haroun recognised the voice of his friend Burayma, a Tuareg boy. They were both fourteen years old and they were good friends. They had both faked their birth certificates to get jobs at Uranico. You were supposed to be at least sixteen to work in the mine.

'*A man with malaria does not swat mosquitoes,*' said Burayma, coming alongside him.

'What are you on about?' said Haroun.

'Look at your boots. They're more hole than boot. Do you think that tucking your trousers into those boots will stop you getting radiation sickness?'

'Just following the chief's instructions,' said Haroun.

'Well don't. We nomads are like sand. We cannot be held in the palm of the hand. If we do everything Gerard says, we are no better than Zermas.'

Haroun chuckled. 'Since you are such a true nomad,' he said, 'tell me how your cows are this afternoon.'

Burayma glowered. He and his family owned no cows and only two camels: an old male called

14

Roosman and a temperamental female called Aghlam.

Haroun laughed and pushed his trolley towards Dynamite Face B.

There were four dynamite faces in the mine and explosions took place twice a week. The miners called these days Deaf Days, because they would go home in the evening with their ears still ringing from the blasts. Blowing uranium rock out of the walls with dynamite was the most efficient way to mine, certainly faster than trying to do it with pickaxes.

Haroun approached Dynamite Face B and saw dozens of distant headlamps darting to and fro like fireflies. Most of the miners here were Zermas, the most numerous tribe in the country as well as the most powerful. Before coming to Tinzar these men had been maize farmers, their arms made strong by years of hoeing the sun-baked soil of Niger. They were not afraid of hard work, and in the Tinzar mine that was exactly what they got.

The mining face was full of holes like a termite mound, and a stick of dynamite had been slotted into each hole. The miners were keeping as far away as possible. Haroun set to work, removing the fuses from each stick of dynamite, sliding them out of their slots in the rock face, and laying them side by side in a wooden crate. These sticks had not exploded when the blast-team detonated them, he told himself, so why should they explode now?

Finished! Haroun turned and stalked off down the tunnel the way he had come. The Zerma miners said nothing but he could feel their eyes on him. When he was out of earshot, then they would talk. The Fulani has courage, they would say. His hands were so steady, they would say, you would have thought he was milking a cow. Or perhaps they would just laugh at him, a gullible Fulani doing a job no one else wanted.

*

It was 8 o'clock by the time Aziz arrived outside the Jeddah National Museum on his motorbike. He parked his motorbike behind a skip, unstrapped the cases from the luggage rack and opened them. He put on the night-vision goggles and took off his clothes. Underneath he was wearing the Synthetic Gecko Skin he had stolen from British Aerospace two years ago. The theft had not been reported in the papers because the very existence of the suit was top secret. It was Aziz's most treasured possession and had already proved useful on several heists.

Aziz placed his left palm on the perimeter wall. It stuck, held fast by millions of tiny molecular forces. He peeled his palm gently off the wall and smiled. Even in this heat, the suit was working perfectly.

He slid his mobile phone into its pouch on his belt, slung the canvas fishing-rod case over his shoulders like a backpack and began to pad up the wall. Place, place, peel and place, the Gecko's movement was fast and fluid and in a moment he was lying flat along the top of the wall.

Down below, a security guard strolled past. Aziz waited five seconds and then skittered headfirst down the wall. Peel and place, peel and place, all the way to the grass below. There was no cover between the perimeter wall and the museum, so he did a fast cat-crawl, keeping low to the ground.

Above him loomed the ornate Arabian façade of the Jeddah National Museum. The Gecko climbed up and in two minutes he was on the roof. There it was – a low metal door which must lead down onto the main stairwell of the museum. He tried the handle. It was locked.

The Gecko liked locked doors. He shrugged the canvas bag off his shoulders, took out his fly pouch and chose the blue fly. He unravelled the fine blue wing-threads to reveal a sliver of metal with a hook on one end and a kink on the other. The blue fly was good salmon bait but an even better lock-pick.

Eleven seconds later the Gecko was standing at the top of the stairwell inside the museum. He scurried up the inside wall and wriggled into a narrow air-vent. A real gecko on the edge of the vent clicked disapprovingly.

Two floors below, a security guard in the Poetry Gallery was about to have the most upsetting night of his life.

*

Haroun finished work at nine o'clock at night and got the shuttle-bus home. Like most Fulanis, Haroun was claustrophobic, and he disliked the shuttle-bus almost as much as the mine. Uranico stripped all the seats out of their buses in order to fit as many miners as possible on each trip to and from Tinzar town. Tonight Haroun was right at the front, pressed against the windscreen by the crush of bodies behind him. He scowled down at the dirt road in the headlights, and at every pothole he braced himself for a bone-crunching jolt.

There was a Toyota pick-up truck in the ditch up ahead, and two orange Yamaha motorbikes nearby, police bikes, by the look of them. There must have been an accident here.

The Toyota had the Uranico colours, white with red markings, and the policemen were busy examining it. As the bus slowed, Haroun caught sight of the registration plate: 4B 9601 RN. That truck belonged to the mine director, Claude Gerard.

The bus stopped and the shouting of the workers gave way to a murmur of consternation. Haroun craned his neck and saw that the driver's window of the truck was smashed.

'What is it?' said Burayma, squashed behind Haroun. 'What are they looking at?'

The bus driver opened his door and got out. Haroun clambered over the driver's seat and stepped down onto the road behind him. The truck had been thoroughly shot up and there was a man slumped over the steering wheel.

'Get back on the bus.' One of the policemen was walking towards them, holding his pistol with both hands. *'Ecoutez-moi!* Back on the bus!'

Haroun was still wearing his helmet-lamp. He flicked it on and peered in through the window of the car. Claude Gerard was dead!

'Back on the bus, Fulani! Do you hear me?'

Gerard had been shot in the neck, chest and stomach. There was blood on the seat and on the dashboard. Haroun looked away, saw the bus-driver hurrying back to his cab, saw the workers on the bus with their noses flattened against the windows. He felt sick.

'Get away from the car!' the policeman shouted, prodding Haroun in the stomach with the barrel of his revolver. Haroun looked again at Gerard's lifeless body. There was blood soaking through the shirt and jacket, blood on the hands and across the side of the seat low down in the shadows. There was almost a pattern to the blood on that seat. It appeared to Haroun like a series of symbols, tiny versions of the brands that African herders mark their cows with.

Haroun stepped away from the car and the angry police officer bustled him back onto the bus. It was unbelievable. Gerard had been murdered!

Burayma was still on the bus with his nose pressed up against the window. He turned to Haroun and scowled. 'Don't say it,' he muttered. 'We do not know who did this thing, so don't say it.'

'It looks like the work of your people,' said Haroun.

'You know nothing!' Burayma shouted. 'I have seen a Zerma stab a Fulani because the Fulani's cow was eating his millet. I have seen a Fulani beat a Zerma because the Zerma shone a torch in his eyes at night. I have seen your own cousins, Haroun, threatening each other with machetes over a girl. So don't stand there and tell me that Tuaregs are the only race of people under heaven with violence in their hearts.'

'I did not say that,' said Haroun. 'But it wouldn't be the first time that Tuareg rebels have killed Uranico workers, would it?'

*

Salif Al-Rawiya had been a security guard all his working life, and the last seven years of those had been spent in the Poetry Gallery of the Jeddah Museum. It was a pleasant place to guard, a splendid high-ceilinged hall which always reminded him of the Grand Mosque in Riyadh. The room was lined with cabinets containing ancient poetry manuscripts from all over the Arabic-speaking world. Displayed across the far wall were the most ancient of them all: the Seven Golden Odes.

The Golden Odes were written by the seven finest poets of the pre-Islamic age and inscribed in gold on seven wide strips of Egyptian linen. They had recently been unearthed in the Arabian desert and now held pride of place in the Jeddah

20

Museum, where visitors flocked to see them. Al-Rawiya himself had read them so often that he could recite all seven by heart.

The hangings were protected by a massive grid of criss-crossing laser alarms, each one strobing up and down about a foot away from the wall. Reaching through the grid to touch one of the hangings would be risky; taking one off the wall without breaking a beam would be impossible. During Al-Rawiya's time at the museum, three people had attempted to steal the Golden Odes. All three were now in Jeddah prison, wishing they had never heard of Golden Odes.

Al-Rawiya watched the orange-red lasers raking up and down, and he smiled. They were beautiful, those lasers, almost as beautiful as the poems themselves. If he had been able to see into the shadowy recess of the air-vent high on the opposite wall, he would have stopped smiling. He would have seen a pair of goggled eyes scrutinising his every move.

After three hours lying in the Poetry Gallery air-vent, Aziz the Human Gecko was well-versed in the paths of the lasers and the routine of the security guard. Every half hour the guard left the room for three minutes to patrol the corridor outside. Aziz had done the calculations. He would need thirty seconds to cross the ceiling, fifteen seconds per poem and thirty seconds back. He would have to be fast. He reached behind his head and switched his goggles onto x4 magnification to examine the handgun in the guard's belt: a 357 Magnum revolver. If he needed an incentive to crawl extra fast tonight, that was it.

The moment the guard turned to leave the Poetry Room, Aziz wriggled forward out of the vent and climbed onto the ceiling, the canvas bag strapped tight on his back. Years of practice had made him an agile upside-down crawler and within thirty seconds he was at the Wall of Golden Odes. He edged down the wall towards the first laser, the blood draining towards his head. There were twelve inches between the alarmed laser curtain and the wall, certainly not enough room for him to crawl into the gap. He would have to do this the hard way.

The Gecko knelt on the wall and faced down towards the linen hangings, held fast by sticky pads on his knees and feet. He opened the canvas bag and assembled the travel rod. Forty-five seconds gone. He clenched the canvas bag between his teeth, steadied the end of the fishing rod between his knees and lowered his line towards the first poem.

Al hamdilillalay! The hook snagged the hanging wire of the first poem. Aziz reeled it in, rolled the linen into a tight scroll and placed it in his bag. He angled the rod sideways and cast his line for the second ode. One minute gone.

One by one, the Gecko hooked the poems and reeled them in, counting time in his head as he fished. One minute thirty seconds. Two minutes. Two minutes thirty seconds. With thirty seconds to go, he reeled in the sixth poem. If he was going to get the seventh poem, he would need to get it first try.

Aziz measured the distance and cast out his line. The silver hook plummeted into the gap between the wall and the laser curtain and as it swung towards the poem's hanging wire Aziz jerked the fishing rod inwards and upwards. The hook missed the wire by an inch and snagged precariously on the linen of the seventh Golden Ode.

'*Subahaanalaahi,*' cursed Aziz. The poem was hooked, but it would surely fall off if he tried to reel it in. He was starting to feel dizzy. Three minutes was a long time to hang upside-down, even for the Gecko.

Fifteen seconds to go. Aziz could hear footsteps in the corridor outside. He twisted his body sideways and flicked the rod backwards over his shoulder. The priceless seventh Golden Ode arced gracefully towards him and was nearly within reach of his outstretched hand when it slipped off the hook and fell.

By the time the linen hanging broke the first laser beam, Aziz had zipped up the canvas bag and pulled it onto his back. By the time it hit the polished wooden floor of the exhibition hall, he was already clambering back up onto the ceiling. An electronic alarm began to scream. The footsteps in the corridor outside broke into a run.

Using only his fingertips and the balls of his feet, Aziz made his way hastily across the ceiling towards his air-vent. There was no way he was going to make it in time. His hand went to the pouch in his belt and fumbled for his phone.

Salif Al-Rawiya ran towards the doorway of the Poetry Gallery, drew his pistol from its holster and flicked the safety catch to off. At Ramadan last year he had caught a Chinese contortionist from the Battambang State Circus trying to skip through the sweeping laser beams without them touching her. He had enjoyed arresting her and he would enjoy arresting this one, whoever it was. He dropped to one knee, steadied his pistol arm with his left hand and swung his body round the lip of the doorway. There was no one in the gallery.

Al-Rawiya stared. Six of the Golden Odes had disappeared and the seventh was lying crumpled on the floor. A fishing rod lay in front of the laser curtain. His eyes darted to the windows. They were locked and undisturbed.

Then he looked up. A man in black was crawling across the ceiling towards the air-vent. Salif Al-Rawiya raised his Magnum and took aim.

'*Salam aleykum!*' he cried.

The thief carried on crawling.

'Stop or I shoot!' shouted Al-Rawiya in Arabic.

The thief stopped. '*Aleykum asalam*,' he said.

'Been fishing?'

The thief nodded.

'Catch any fish?'

'Six,' said the thief.

'Time to throw them back.'

24

'I can't do that! They're for my supper!'

Something exploded two floors above them and all the lights went out.

The Gecko peeled his hands off the ceiling and stood up so that he was hanging upside-down by the soles of his feet. A shot ricocheted off the ceiling plaster in front of him, another behind him. He could hear the guard below shouting to his colleagues for a torch.

Aziz smiled. He had taken the precaution of putting a C4 'blowfly' in the fusebox on the third floor. He had detonated it from his mobile phone and blown the lights. Now he reached behind his head and switched his goggles to night mode. He walked calmly to the air-vent and slid inside.

*

It was late at night by the time Haroun arrived home. The cows were lying down around the huts. One or two were sleeping, but most were chewing the cud, swishing their tails back and forth to drive away mosquitoes.

No sound came from his parents' hut. Outside the entrance of the other hut, his brother Hamma was fast asleep, the hood of his black shepherd's cloak pulled up over his face. Haroun lay down beside him and stared up at the stars.

Haroun, listen to me, I believe Monsieur Gerard is in danger. The *tuubaaku* who called himself Remy had *known* that this would happen. And neither Gerard nor Haroun had listened to him. *There are bad things going on at the mine.*

A mosquito whined in Haroun's ears. He pulled the tightly-rolled turban out from under his brother's head and draped it over his own. The whine of the mosquito went away.

Tomorrow morning I will go and see the tuubaaku at the nomadic library. I will not leave until he has answered all my questions.

3

'*Dites-moi, Tuubaaku, comment tu savais?* How did you know that Monsieur Gerard was in danger?' In his anger, Haroun's French was surprisingly fluent.

'Calm down, Haroun,' whispered Remy. 'We cannot talk until the last child has left the library.'

It was eight o'clock in the morning and the *Bibliothèque Nomadique* was parked outside the Tinzar primary school for nomads. The double doors at the back of the lorry were open and there was a ramp for getting in and out. Inside, the lorry was lined with shelves, and a queue of wide-eyed Fulani and Tuareg children was passing through, each one choosing his or her book for the week. Remy was sitting on a stool at the bottom of the ramp, writing a list of names and books.

In years gone by, Haroun's father had sent him to a nomadic school like this one, because the school gave each child a free bowl of couscous at lunchtime. It was there that Haroun had learned to speak French. He had wanted to continue his studies at the local *lycée*, but his father could not afford the fees. *There is no point sending you there,* his father had said. *They teach you nothing about cows and they don't even give you couscous.*

The children filed out of the library and returned to their classroom clutching their borrowed books. Haroun squatted down next to Remy's stool. His initial anger had subsided but he was still upset.

'*Alors,*' he said, 'how did you know?'

Remy sighed. 'There was a letter. Three weeks ago your director Claude Gerard wrote to his brother in France. In that letter he said that he had learned of something bad going on at the Tinzar mine. He was planning to resign and return to France.'

'What do you mean, something bad?' asked Haroun.

'*Les activités dangereuses,*' said Remy. 'Those were his exact words. Tinzar is a uranium mine, Haroun. Can you imagine just how terrible those "dangerous activities" might be?'

Haroun nodded. 'What did Gerard's brother do when he got the letter?'

'He was worried. He showed me the letter and I told him I would come and talk to Gerard. Find out more.'

'You are a friend of the family?'

Remy looked down at Haroun and his eyes narrowed. 'You told me it is shameful to ask a lot of questions.'

Haroun nodded. 'In that case, let me tell you a

story.' He placed an index finger in the sand and drew the shape of a violin. 'In the kingdom of Liptaako, there was a travelling violinist called Faruk. Whenever he arrived at a new village, Faruk would ask for the house of the richest man in the village. He would squat outside the rich man's gate and play his violin, and from time to time the rich man would come out of his house and give Faruk a cola nut or a beaker of coffee. With me so far?'

'Yes.'

'Faruk would sit outside that rich man's gate for three days and three nights and then he would move on to the next rich man at the next village. And one day each of those rich men would come back from the mosque to find the door of his house gone and all his possessions gone with it.'

'I see,' said Remy. 'Faruk had told someone where to go and when to break in.'

'That's right, *Tuubaaku*. Faruk was the first but he was not the last. I tell you the truth, every thief in Tinzar prison has a brother who is either a violinist, a shoe-shiner or a medicine pedlar.'

'*Les éspions*,' said Remy softly. 'Spies.'

'*Exactement*. The spies of Africa.'

Silence.

'I am no violinist,' said Remy.

'Correct,' said Haroun. 'You are a book pedlar.' The white man laughed. 'I have never lied to you.'

'And neither have you told me the truth,' said Haroun. 'So, are you a friend of Monsieur Gerard's family?'

'I am not,' said Remy. 'I work for the French government. Uranico is a French company, you see. It is essential that we find out what dangerous activities are going on at the Tinzar mine, and why Monsieur Gerard was killed.'

'You are a spy,' said Haroun.

Remy looked at his feet. 'If you insist on using that word, then yes, I am a spy.'

Haroun nodded. 'We Fulani have a proverb,' he said. '*Bannde bunndu wanaa fijorde bumdo*. The mouth of a well is no place for a blind man to play.'

'I'll bear that in mind,' said Remy. 'Will you help me or not?'

Haroun said nothing. Being a miner in Tinzar exposed him to quite enough danger already. How much greater that danger would be if he turned spy! Besides, whoever killed Gerard would not hesitate to kill again.

'Do you know what this is?' Remy held out a small black box with a silver screen.

'No.'

'It's a GPS receiver. With one of these you will never again get lost in the desert.'

'I am a Fulani,' said Haroun. 'I never get lost.'

'What about these?' The white man held out a tiny camera and a mobile phone. 'They are yours, if you want them.'

Haroun tried to look like he did not care. 'I do not know how to use such things,' he said.

'I can teach you,' said Remy. 'Haroun, I need a man in the mine. Will you help me or not?'

Haroun bit his lip. The *tuubaaku* was using

expensive gifts as bait to hook his fish. It was a shameful way to behave.

'Will you help me?' repeated Remy.

Haroun looked up and met the white man's eyes. 'Okay,' he said. 'What do you want me to do?'

*

● http://www.reunitedfriends.fr/chat/member7586758/

ReunitedFriends.fr
chat

You are logged in as *Zabri*.
Your old friend *Agahan* **is online.**
Chat? <u>YES</u> I <u>NO</u> YES

ZABRI:	*Salam aleykum.*
AGAHAN:	*Aleykum asalam.* Fifty years ago, what did the imajaghan desire?
ZABRI:	**Fast dromedary, red saddle, sword and song of love.**
AGAHAN:	And today?
ZABRI:	**Plate of rice, blanket, souvenir sword.**
AGAHAN:	Have you arrived back in Niger?
ZABRI:	**Yes. We're at the lab.**
AGAHAN:	How is the Baker?
ZABRI:	**He keeps asking for his Golden Odes.**
AGAHAN:	The Gecko will bring you the odes tomorrow. Give the Baker only the first two: the Ode of Amr and the Ode of Antar.
ZABRI:	**And the rest?**
AGAHAN:	Later. Give him something to work towards. *Salam aleykum.*
ZABRI:	*Aleykum asalam.*

Remy was as good as his word. He spent the next hour and a half teaching Haroun to use the camera and phone. He even showed him how to connect the two and attach photos to a text message. As the sun neared its zenith, they went up to the top of a nearby dune and took pictures of cows and goats grazing on the plains below.

'Why did Gerard refuse to talk to you?' said Haroun suddenly.

Remy looked around him sharply, but here on the dune there was no chance of being overheard. 'I met with Gerard the night before he was killed,' he said. 'I am sure he wanted to talk, but he wanted to do so in his own time. His own time never arrived.'

'We Fulani have a proverb,' said Haroun. '*Si deddaado wi'i jam suroobe pornyoo.* If he who is being strangled says "Peace", his rescuers will turn back.'

Remy nodded. 'You can't force your help on someone who doesn't want it.'

Haroun sat down and looked towards the east, where the Shinn Massif, a vast range of black-topped mountains, loomed. If dead men could talk, he wondered, what would Claude Gerard tell them about the Tinzar uranium mine? What had he found out which had so rattled him?

'If only he had written more in that letter,' said Remy.

If only he had written more . . . an image flashed across Haroun's mind, nine symbols drawn in blood on the side of a seat, low down in the shadows where only the most observant would notice them. Haroun drew a straight line in the sand, followed by three dots and a circle.

$$|\vdots \bigcirc$$

Remy looked. 'What are those?'

'Cattle brands,' said Haroun. 'I saw nine cattle brands drawn in blood on Gerard's seat.'

'Cattle brands?' Remy crouched down to get a closer look. 'What are they?'

'Every herder has a brand that he uses to mark his cows, in case they get lost. Each has a different shape.'

Remy leaned forward. 'Haroun, I need you to draw all the symbols you saw, exactly as you saw them. Can you do that?'

Haroun drew in the sand, slowly and carefully:

$$|\vdots \bigcirc \qquad \bullet = \qquad \} \odot = +$$

'You're sure?' said Remy.

'A Fulani herder does not forget a brand,' said Haroun. 'But there are a couple here that I've never seen before.'

Remy's eyes brightened and he jumped up. 'Those symbols may look like cattle brands,' he said, 'but they are not!' He jumped up and ran off down the dune, plunging deep into the sand with every stride.

Haroun got up and followed. He wished that the Frenchman would act in a calmer and more honourable way. Rushing away from a conversation was the behaviour of a child.

He found Remy back in the library van, poring over a large book. The Frenchman's white hands trembled as he leafed through the pages.

'There!' said Remy, thrusting the book under Haroun's nose.

On the open page was a column of symbols, including the ones Haroun had just drawn.

'It's called Tifinagh,' said Remy. 'It was an ancient Tamasheq alphabet.'

'I've heard of it,' said Haroun. 'And Monsieur Gerard loved African languages. He probably had a copy of that same book.'

Haroun ran his eyes up and down the column of strange symbols and quickly deciphered Gerard's dying words.

'*Năghăra aw yeswita,*' he said. 'I know some Tamasheq but I don't recognise those words.'

'Lucky we have a dictionary,' smiled Remy, running his finger down a page. 'Let me see . . . no . . . *Năghăra* is not here.'

Haroun grabbed the dictionary and flicked through it. 'Neither is *yeswita.*'

'So much for loving the local languages,' said Remy. 'It looks as though Claude Gerard wasted his dying moments writing gobbledygook.'

Haroun sighed. 'What now?'

'Maybe the new director of Uranico will give us some answers.'

'Blaise Soda?' Haroun looked up in amazement. 'You are going to walk into Soda's office and ask him what kind of *activités dangereuses* are going on in the mine? He'll eat you alive.'

'In that case,' said Remy, 'we will have to use this.'

He held out a hand. On his palm lay a tiny silver clip.

'What is it?' said Haroun.

'A surge clip,' said Remy. 'Let me show you how it works.'

*

Haroun hitched a lift to the mine and went to the Administration Block. Blaise Soda was now Acting Director and had already moved into Monsieur Gerard's old office. Haroun raised his hand to knock, then hesitated. Between Dynamite Face B and Blaise Soda's lair, he would choose the Dynamite Face any day of the week.

'*Entrez!*' came the shrill voice within. Soda must have seen him through the frosted glass in his door.

Haroun entered the office and looked around. He had been in this room twice before and it had not changed, except that Gerard's map of West Africa had been taken down and replaced with a poster entitled 'Deadly Creatures of the World'. Beneath the poster sat Blaise Soda, his revolting ferret perched on his shoulder.

'You,' said Soda irritably. 'What do you want?'

Haroun took a deep breath. 'I need new boots,' he said. 'These ones are not safe.'

'Not safe?' Soda's lip curled. 'Take them off.'

'What?'

'Take off your boots and place them on the desk in front of me.'

Haroun did as he was told. Soda took the left boot and held it up in front of him.

'Tell me,' said Soda, 'what is unsafe about this boot?'

'It is full of holes,' said Haroun. 'I am afraid of the radiation.'

Soda opened a drawer in his desk and took out a plastic tube with a dial on it. There were lots of these instruments around the mining compound; it was a Geiger counter, used to measure radioactivity.

Soda passed the Geiger counter over the boot and it began to click slowly. This was an average level of radiation, not immediately harmful.

The director turned and passed the Geiger counter over the 'Deadly Creatures' poster on the wall behind him – the clicks continued at the same rate. Then he took the ferret off his shoulder and passed the counter over it. Still the same level of radioactivity.

'How does my ferret look to you?' he said to Haroun in his most sarcastic voice. Haroun cast an eye over the animal's mangy fur and toothy grin.

'Fine,' said Haroun.

'She's not glowing?'

'No.'

'Not teetering on the brink of death?'

'No.'

'Well then, Fulani, so long as Fifi lives and breathes and catches mice, you'll be fine as well.'

Blaise Soda put the Geiger counter back in its drawer and turned his attention back to Haroun's boot. He turned it over and picked a burr out of the sole.

'This burr,' he said, 'where is it from?'

Haroun did not answer. *Clever man*, he thought. Unpleasant, but without a doubt clever.

'I did not see any burr bushes down in the mine the last time I was there,' continued Soda. 'Tell me, Fulani, do you by any chance wear these boots when you are out herding your goats?'

'Cows,' said Haroun in a small voice. He backed away from Soda until he could go no further. His hands behind his back were touching the wall, feeling around for the electric cable that led up to the strip light on the office ceiling.

'I see,' said Soda slowly. 'You wear your Uranico boots – company property – to herd your cows in the bush, and then you have the NERVE to come in here and complain to ME that the boots are FULL OF HOLES. I call that VERY RUDE.'

'Sorry,' said Haroun.

'GET OUT,' roared Soda, 'and TAKE THESE WITH YOU!'

Haroun dodged the first boot but the second caught him on the side of his head and almost knocked him over. He picked them up and scuttled towards the door.

Soda grinned as he watched the boy leave.

This was his first day in charge and already he had asserted his authority. He began to play back the conversation in his head, congratulating himself on his sarcasm and wit.

Then he remembered something which made him frown in puzzlement. *I am afraid of the radiation* – had the boy really said that? Fulanis were never afraid. And if the boy was *not* afraid of radiation, *why had he come to the office*?

Blaise Soda began to swivel round and round in his office chair, thinking furiously. His ferret jumped into his lap and then scampered up his arm to sit on his shoulder. Faster and faster man and ferret spun.

Suddenly the strip light on the ceiling flickered and went out. Soda grabbed the edge of the desk and jolted to a standstill; the ferret flew off at a tangent with a little shriek. The director tutted. He got up and raised the blinds on the one small window in his office, letting in some light. Then he took out his mobile and dialled.

'Maintenance? Soda here. I need a light replaced. Do it quickly.'

Haroun was in the Maintenance Department loading light bulbs into his trolley when his boss Rahiim called him over. Rahiim was an elderly Zerma who had worked here since the mine's beginnings more than forty years ago.

'Haroun, I've just had a call from Soda. He needs a strip light replacing. Can you do that before you go underground?'

Haroun's heart pounded as he pushed his

trolley back to the Administration Block. Soda stood in the doorway, arms folded.

'Why did you come here just now?' said Soda.

Haroun looked at him blankly and said nothing. Playing dumb was the only way through this.

The director stood aside for him. 'I'm watching you, Fulani,' he said as Haroun went past him into the office.

Haroun set up his little stepladder and climbed up to unscrew the old strip light from its holder. Under the cold gaze of Blaise Soda he replaced it with a new one from his trolley. Then he went to the light-switch and turned it on; the light began to flicker into life. With his free hand he slipped a tiny silver clip off the cable leading to the light. Remy's surge clip had worked perfectly.

'Now get out of here,' said Soda. 'If I see you again today you're fired.'

Haroun packed up his stepladder, put the dud light into his trolley and trundled off.

Soda's white Toyota pick-up was parked outside the Administration Block. Haroun took a small black box out of his trolley, glanced left and right and opened up the bonnet of Soda's truck. He clipped the box onto the side of the car battery and attached the wires as Remy had told him: red to red, black to black. The tiny bug in the new strip light did not have enough power to transmit long distances; it needed the help of an amplifier connected to a secondary power source like a car battery. So long as the amplifier stayed close to the bug, it could transmit its signal up to two kilometres.

Planting the amplifier took just twelve seconds. Haroun shut the bonnet and turned to see a tall Zerma miner watching him.

'Car bomb?' said the miner.

'Maintenance,' said Haroun, showing his ID card. 'But a bomb is not a bad idea. Maybe next time.'

The two employees chuckled, shook hands and walked off in opposite directions. When he was out of earshot, Haroun permitted himself a long sigh of relief. His first mission was accomplished: Blaise Soda's office was bugged.

4

At the end of his shift Haroun took the shuttle-bus back to Tinzar. He closed his eyes as he passed the place where Claude Gerard had been murdered, and did not open them again until the bus stopped in Tahala.

Tahala lay exactly halfway between the mine itself and the town of Tinzar. It was an artificial village that Uranico had built to accommodate its miners. Haroun could have lived there too, but he preferred the quietness of the bush and the closeness of his cows.

The driver started the engine again and the bus drove off towards Tinzar. When it arrived at the *gare*, Haroun got down and sidled off into the dark criss-crossing streets of Tinzar town. He hurried through the maze of mud-brick houses and narrow dusty streets, glancing behind him now and then to make sure he was not being followed. On either side, turbaned men crouched in the dim orange light of their paraffin lamps, pouring tea and talking in low guttural voices.

Haroun went past the mosque and then ducked through a low archway into a narrow corridor. A boy lounging in a broken deckchair held out his hand and Haroun gave him the entrance fee of one hundred francs. The corridor opened out into a yard full of chairs where a crowd of men was watching football. In front of them was a satellite dish and a huge television on a metal stand.

Haroun took a place in the back row next to a man in a copious black turban. The turban was pulled up over the man's mouth and the top half of the face was covered by a large pair of sunglasses.

'*Salam aleykum*,' hissed Haroun.

'*Aleykum asalam*,' replied the man. The television commentary was so loud that they had to lean their heads towards each other to hear.

'What's the match?' said Haroun.

'Chelsea Barcelona,' said the man.

'Nice turban. You look like a true *imajaghan*.'

'What's that?'

'A Tuareg noble.'

Remy chuckled.

'The microphone I planted in Soda's office,' said Haroun, 'is it working?'

'Perfectly.'

GOAL! A deafening cheer filled the tent. Dozens of young turbanned men clapped and stamped and one fellow in the front row stood up and waved his chair above his head.

'So,' said Haroun, 'has he said anything interesting?'

'Lots,' said Remy. 'Come and sit here, Fifi. You're beautiful, Fifi. I love you, Fifi. Tell me, Haroun, who is this Fifi woman and why does she never say anything?'

Haroun clicked his tongue against the roof of his mouth. Amongst the Fulani, it was shameful for a man to be overheard speaking affectionately even to his own wife. To a ferret it was appalling!

'She's Soda's ferret,' he said. 'She goes everywhere with him and likes to sit on his shoulder. Soda's crazy about her.'

Remy laughed. 'He's crazy all right.'

'So is that all?' asked Haroun. 'He didn't mention any of his *activités dangereuses*?'

'There was one thing. Soda received a telephone call at about five o'clock which made him nervous. He told whoever it was never to call him at work and asked them to call him at home tonight. They must have told him that tonight was no good, because he then said, "Tomorrow night then."'

Haroun was worried. 'Why not talk to them at work? Does he suspect his office is bugged?'

'No,' said Remy. 'He's just being careful. Some-one could be listening outside the window, or by the door. At home he knows he is on his own.'

'So what do we do?'

'You bug his house.'

'When?' asked Haroun, making an effort to keep his voice steady.

'That depends,' said Remy, 'on whether or not you want to see the end of this match.'

Haroun suddenly wanted very much to see the end of the match. Anything to postpone breaking into Blaise Soda's home.

'*Bernde feewa teppere feewa kaa walaa*,' said Haroun. 'You cannot have a cool heel and a cool heart.'

Remy took off his sunglasses and raised a quizzical eyebrow.

'If you run your own errands,' explained Haroun, 'your feet will heat up, because you're walking all the time. But if you send someone else to run your errands for you, your heart will heat up because they'll get something wrong and you'll end up being mad at them.'

Remy laughed. 'I see,' he said. 'You want me to do my own dirty work. On this occasion it is impossible, Haroun; I don't have a Uranico uniform, and yours wouldn't fit me. Surely you are not afraid of a man who spends his days telling his pet ferret how much he loves it?'

'I'm not afraid of anything,' said Haroun. 'I just thought you might want to do it. You're the spy, after all.'

'Oooooh,' gasped the crowd as a thirty-metre shot grazed the top of the crossbar.

'Take this,' said Remy, passing an envelope to Haroun. 'Put it out of sight, as close to the telephone as possible.'

Haroun shook his head. 'Tinzar and Tahala do not have telephone lines. Everyone uses mobiles.'

'Oh. In that case, put it as close to Soda's mobile as possible.'

'You mean in his pocket? Fine. I'll do that, and you go and inform all the vultures and hyenas of Tinzar that if they come to Tahala tonight they'll find a dead Fulani.'

Remy chuckled. 'You will find a way, Haroun.'

GOAL!! Chelsea had equalised from a corner. A section of the audience leapt to their feet and danced for joy. As Haroun got up to leave, the Frenchman handed him a heavy carrier bag. 'These are for you.'

Haroun went back through the corridor and ducked through the arch into the labyrinth of streets outside. When he reached the shadow of the mosque, he opened the bag. Inside was a pair of shiny new boots.

*

Walking along the main road to Tahala miners' village should have taken Haroun less than half an hour, but instead he took a roundabout route through the desert. He did not want to risk being seen by any vehicles that might be on the road.

It was late at night when he arrived. The miners' village was surrounded by a high electric fence and the front gate was the only way in and out. Haroun swaggered in through the gate and waved at the two security guards who were playing cards under a streetlight. One of the guards started to get up but when he saw Haroun's Uranico uniform he sat down again.

Tahala was a grid of well-lit streets, very different from the alleys of Tinzar that Haroun

45

had just come from. One central shopping street divided the town into two halves – rich and poor. The poor side was for the miners and consisted of long rows of mud-brick houses roofed with corrugated iron. The rich side consisted of whitewashed villas for office workers and the mine director himself. Here were mango trees, bougainvillea bushes, stone fountains and elaborately-carved wooden benches. The security measures were also elaborate – each house had its own guard and its own set of security lights, triggered by the slightest movement.

That morning Blaise Soda had moved into Monsieur Gerard's villa with his two wives and seven children. Haroun hopped over the back fence into the garden and immediately found himself caught in the full beam of a security light. He ran across the grass and swung himself up into the branches of a mango tree just as the night guard came round the corner of the house.

The security guard strode across the lawn, passing right beneath the mango tree. He started shining his torch into the bougainvillea bushes which lined the fence.

Haroun saw his opportunity. While the guard's back was turned, he shinned down the tree and ran round the side of the house. All of the windows were firmly closed. There was no way in.

At the front of the house, Haroun saw the security guard's armchair and a carport with Soda's white Toyota pick-up truck parked underneath it. He darted into the carport and crouched behind the car right next to Soda's front door. The carport was a rough trellis covered in creepers.

The guard returned to his chair outside the carport and Haroun squatted inside, hardly daring to breathe. He could see the guard through the gaps in the latticework and he noticed a holster hanging from his belt.

Haroun tried the handle of the front door and found it locked. Then he noticed a little flap low down in the door, just big enough for a cat. Or a ferret. He lifted the flap and peered in. The hallway was dark, but there was a chink of light under one of the adjoining doors. He heard a woman's voice raised in anger:

'So you'll happily pay for Haibata's children to go to Agadez *lycée*, but mine have to make do with that shack of a school here in Tahala, is that it?'

'You know it's not like that, dear.' Blaise Soda sounded stressed. 'I can't afford for all *seven* to go to Agadez, can I?'

'Can't you? You are director now! You said that if you ever became director—'

'Hamsetu, that's enough! We will talk about this tomorrow.'

'Tomorrow, tomorrow, always tomorrow. And meanwhile poverty slithers all over us like a carpet viper and squeezes the life out of us.'

'Carpet vipers don't squeeze, dear. They bite.'

'Well so do I, *dear*, so just you watch out!'

Haroun put his arm through the flap and reached up as far as he could inside the door. The key was not in the lock. There was no way Soda's mobile phone was going to be bugged tonight, but there was no way out either. Haroun was trapped between a locked door and an armed guard. If Soda or one of his wives were to come out of the front door at this moment, they would walk right into him.

He crouched in the darkness and waited. Perhaps the guard would get up and take a walk, allowing him to make his getaway. Half an hour passed. One hour. Two hours. The guard did not move except to cross and uncross his legs. *Ko jemma boni fuu, na weetu,* thought Haroun. Even if the night is bad, morning will come.

The flap in the front door swung open and Haroun found himself face to face with Blaise Soda's ferret. She stood half in and half out of the flap, grinning toothily and assessing the situation.

Haroun grinned back at her, remembering Remy's confusion when he listened to the bug in Soda's office. *Who is this Fifi? She's Soda's ferret. She goes everywhere with him and likes to sit on his shoulder.* Haroun looked at Fifi's pink collar and an idea formed in his mind. *She likes to sit on his shoulder.* Perhaps tonight's escapade would not be entirely wasted.

Haroun opened his palm towards the ferret and clicked his tongue in quiet welcome, whilst his other hand felt in his pocket for the envelope that Remy had given him. The bug in the envelope was no bigger than a button, even smaller than the one they had put in Soda's strip light. Haroun took out a small tube of superglue and squeezed some glue onto the back of the button. The ferret blinked her beady eyes and tiptoed forward to investigate. Haroun waited until she was well within reach and then made a grab for her collar. If he could not bug Soda's phone tonight, he would at least make sure he bugged Soda's ferret.

The startled ferret yelped and struggled to get away, but Haroun tightened his grip. Through a gap in the trellis he saw the security guard get out of his chair and move towards the carport. Haroun acted quickly. He stuck the bug firmly onto the inside of Fifi's collar, jumped into the back of the pick-up truck, lay down and pulled a piece of tarpaulin over himself. Haroun heard the guard come into the carport, heard him walk around the truck, saw the beam of a torch sweeping to and fro. He held his breath.

'It's *you*, is it?' said the guard. 'You scared me, you daft animal.'

The footsteps retreated and Haroun heard the quiet swish of the ferret-flap.

The bug was in the house. It was attached to Soda's ferret and powered by Soda's own car battery. Whenever Fifi was within fifty metres of her master's truck, the collar microphone would transmit. Cheeky, thought Haroun, but very neat indeed.

*

ROOM 101
CHATCHATCHAT ☕

Please enter your username: Agahan
Please enter your password: tiwse

There is [1] person in # Room 101.
Enter? **YES** I <u>NO</u>   **YES**

Welcome to Room 101, *Agahan*. *Zabri* is here.

Zabri:	***Salam aleykum*. Fast camel, red saddle, sword and song.**
Agahan:	*Aleykum asalam*. And today?
Zabri:	**Plate of rice, blanket, sword.**
Agahan:	Did the Baker like the poems you gave him?
Zabri:	**Too much. He cried when he saw The Golden Ode of Antar.**
Agahan:	Has he started baking?
Zabri:	**Yes. But he says we need much more cake.**
Agahan:	*Subahaanalaahi.*

*

'How did you get out?' said Remy, having listened wide-eyed to Haroun's account of the night's adventure.

'I lay in the back of the truck until morning,' said Haroun. 'When the sun rose, the night guard got up and left, so I got up and left, too.'

'Good,' said Remy. 'Tonight I will drive out to the desert behind Tahala and from there I can listen to—' He broke off abruptly. The children of Boosuma School for Nomads were beginning to file into the library. 'Go and find yourself a good book,' said Remy. 'I must work now.'

Haroun mingled with the children from the nomadic school and began to browse the shelves of the library. He found a heavy book about the Tamasheq language which included a chapter about that ancient writing system Tifinagh. He went outside, sat down on the sand, leant back against one of the massive wheels of the mobile library and laboriously began to read:

'Tifinagh is the traditional Tamasheq alphabet. It is a consonantal script derived from Phoenician and it dates back over 2000 years. It can be written left-to-right or right-to-left.'

Right-to-left. Haroun stared. Tifinagh could be written from right to left! Remy had not known that. The question was, had Monsieur Gerard?

Haroun dashed into the library, grabbed the Tamasheq-French dictionary and dashed back out. He knelt in the sand and scrawled Gerard's Tifinagh message in front of him.

$$ \text{I} \equiv \bigcirc \quad \bullet = \quad \text{}\rangle \odot = + $$

Reading from left to right, the message had made no sense. But reading from right to left, it said – Haroun looked up the letters one by one –

tiwse wa ărăghăn. He thumbed through the dictionary, his fingers shaking. There it was!

Tiwse: annual tribute (tax) traditionally paid to the Tuareg supreme chief

Haroun licked his lips and searched for the second word.

Wa: the / that / the one that

Now for the third word.

Ărăghăn: yellow

'*Tiwse wa ărăghăn*' murmured Haroun. 'Tribute that is yellow. *Yellow tribute!*'

He sat back against the wheel and gazed at the horizon. *Yellow tribute.* What the *zorki* was that?

5

'What do you know about tribute, Burayma?'

It was afternoon in the Uranico mine. Haroun and his Tuareg friend were strolling along Gallery F8. Haroun was supposed to be looking for broken light bulbs and Burayma was supposed to be far away in Gallery B17.

'I wish everyone would shut up about tribute,' said Burayma. 'Tribute is ancient history.'

'What do you mean? Who else has been talking to you about tribute?'

'My uncle, for one. He was saying just last night that I should not be working down a mine. He said that the *imajaghan* used to be great rulers and warriors. They lived by raiding other tribes and stealing their animals.'

Haroun laughed. 'Your uncle doesn't want you to do that, does he?'

'Of course not. He just wants me to remember that I'm of noble stock.'

'Noble!' cried Haroun. 'Those *imajaghan* were parasites.'

'They were free spirits,' said Burayma. 'And they didn't raid everyone. Some villages they protected in return for tribute.'

'Which was what?'

'Cows. Crops. Gold. Whatever their subjects had, they would give a portion to the *imajaghan*.'

Gold, thought Haroun. *Yellow tribute*. He wanted to know more, but he knew he would have to tread very carefully indeed.

'What about now?' he said airily.

'What do you mean?'

'Do you think the *imajaghan* still receive tribute?'

'If we did,' Burayma said, 'do you think I would be working down here? Do you think my brother would be a tour guide? Do you think my uncle Seydou would be begging in Mecca? Of course we don't receive tribute.'

'That's okay then,' said Haroun. 'So you promise not to come a-raiding my cows?'

'Why would I want your cows? They all have scabies.'

'They do not!'

Haroun punched Burayma on the side of the head, slightly harder than he had meant to. Like a flash Burayma grabbed him, knocked him over and sat on him. Pinned down on the floor of the tunnel, Haroun felt the cold groundwater soaking through his overalls.

'You're quite quick for a Tuareg,' he said.

'And you're quite ugly for a Fulani,' rejoined Burayma.

The time had come to ask the question Haroun had been leading up to.

'What about the rebels?' he said innocently. 'Do they receive tribute from anyone?'

Burayma stiffened. 'How should I know?' he said. 'My family has nothing to do with the rebels. Anyway it's none of your business. I must go – I'm supposed to be in B17.' He jumped up and hurried away.

'Look at that,' said Haroun, gazing up at the tunnel ceiling. 'There's a light bulb that needs changing.'

*

That night Haroun got off the shuttle-bus at Tahala, but instead of going through the front gate with the other miners, he turned and walked east into the desert. He glanced back and saw Burayma standing at one of the windows of the bus, watching him. Was that shame in his eyes? Or was it fear?

There was a crescent moon and Haroun could see the faint line of the horizon where the desert met the sky. Far away two tiny lights flashed once. He walked towards them. Again the lights flashed, clearly recognisable now as the headlights of a vehicle. The *Bibliothèque Nomadique* was far from home.

'*Oss, oss,*' cried Haroun as he approached the library. He opened one of the back doors and climbed in.

Inside the vehicle the only light came from a

large flat computer screen. Remy was sitting in front of it, wearing a pair of headphones. Haroun stared. That very morning there had been no screen there, only bookshelves.

'*Fermez la porte,*' said the Frenchman sharply, without looking at him. Haroun closed the door.

'Where are the bookshelves?' asked Haroun.

'The middle sections on this side pull out and slide back,' said Remy. 'It's useful for when I want to watch DVDs.'

'Or eavesdrop on a ferret,' said Haroun. 'Has Soda received that telephone call, yet?'

'I don't know,' said Remy. 'Your blasted ferret keeps wandering off.'

'Where is she now?'

'She's with Soda. Listen.'

Remy threw him some headphones and motioned to the stool next to him. Haroun sat down. The computer screen had a thick line across the middle of it which shimmered and leapt and made his eyes feel funny.

'What's that?' he asked.

'That's the sound wave being transmitted from the ferret mic,' said Remy. 'Welcome to Fifi's world.'

Haroun put the headphones on.

'*What are you doing?*' said Blaise Soda loudly in his ear. Haroun whipped the headphones off and spun round to face his enemy. There was no one there.

Remy chuckled. 'Not used to headphones, are you?' he said. Haroun shook his head and whistled through his teeth. He put the headphones back on, slowly this time.

'*What are you doing, Fifi?*' said Blaise Soda. '*Stop it, I'm trying to read. Stop it, I say.*'

'*Blaise,*' said a woman's voice, '*when will you give me a necklace like the one you gave Hamsetu?*'

'*I gave you a necklace, Haibata.*'

'*Not like Hamsetu's. Hers has diamonds in it.*'

'*That's glass, Haibata, not real diamonds.*'

'*Mine doesn't even have glass in it.*'

'*Yours is silver.*'

'*I hate silver. All the jewellery in this town is silver. Silver, silver, silver, silver, silver, silv—*'

'*Haibata!*'

'*What?*'

'*I'm trying to read.*'

Soda's ring-tone started up – an annoying monophonic jingle. With any luck this would be the telephone call they had been waiting for. Remy clicked on a small red circle at the top of the screen. The words 'NOW RECORDING' appeared next to it.

'*Go into the kitchen, Haibata. This call is important.*'

Haroun heard some loud throat-clearing and then a click.

'*Bonsoir. This is Soda.*'

There was a short pause, then a gentle male voice spoke. '*Salam aleykum.*'

'*Aleykum asalam. Are you passing the evening in peace, monsieur?*'

'*Peace only,*' said the voice. '*How do you like your new job?*'

'*It pleases me very well.*'

'*Good. We need to ta—*'

The voice faded away suddenly.

'*Sacré bleu*,' muttered Remy. 'Can your blasted ferret not stay in one place for five seconds? You should have put some of that glue on its paws as well as its collar.'

Silence. Then:

'*What do you mean, they're not real diamonds?*' The new voice in Haroun's ears was a woman's. Remy put his head in his hands and groaned.

'*Blaise just told me. It's glass, he said. That necklace I gave Hamsetu is a worthless trinket, he said. He was laughing as he said it.*'

Remy was beside himself with anxiety. 'We're missing the call,' he muttered. 'Get back to your master, you mangy, rat-faced—'

Hamsetu's shriek of horror drowned out Remy's opinion of Soda's ferret. '*No! Blaise told me they were priceless gems from the Chinti-chin-chin diamond mines in Outer Mongolia. That lying son of an aardvark.*'

Haroun smiled. *That's right, Hamsetu*, he thought. *Get angry. Kick the ferret.*

'*How dare he give me a glass necklace, as if I were an empty-headed Fulani milkmaid! That cheap, worthless, lying . . .*'

Kick the ferret, breathed Haroun.

'*What do you think you're looking at, you buck-toothed louse-infested furball! Get out of my sight!*'

Haroun heard the sound he had been hoping for: the squashy thud of foot on fur, the ferrety yelp and the scampering of paws. He knew that the frightened animal would head straight to the place she felt safest – her master's shoulder.

He was right.

'What's wrong, my darling?' Soda's voice again. *'No, Monsieur, I wasn't talking to you. I was talking to my—'*

'Soda, do we have a deal or not?'

'Yes, Monsieur, we have a deal.'

'Alors – Salam aleykum.'

'Aleykum asalam.'

A soft click and then silence, broken only by Fifi's fretful chattering.

Remy was shaking his head. 'Four hours of surveillance,' he said, 'and this happens.'

'At least Fifi got a good kick,' said Haroun.

The Frenchman took off his headphones and stretched. The sound wave on the computer screen continued to leap up and down; Hamsetu was almost certainly notifying her husband of her thoughts on the subject of glass jewellery.

'Spying is like that,' said Remy, raking his fingers through his hair. 'You risk everything to plant a decent bug and end up being shafted by a ferret.'

'It's not like we haven't learned anything,' said Haroun.

Remy looked at him with tired eyes. 'Really? What have you learned?'

'The caller is someone Soda respects and fears. He called to negotiate with Soda, probably to confirm or modify a deal they made before Gerard's death.'

'Guesswork,' said Remy.

'The caller is a middle-aged Tuareg,' said Haroun.

'How can you possibly know that?'

'The ends of the words *accord* and *alors*; he said them deep down in his throat, as if his mother tongue was either Arabic or Tamasheq. There are not many Arabs in the north of Niger, so he's probably a Tuareg.'

'Guesswork,' said Remy again. 'We don't even know the call came from Niger.'

'It came from right here in Tinzar,' said Haroun. 'The silversmith's workshop in sector 5, behind the Wahhabist prayer house.'

Remy stared. 'Don't goof around, boy. This is serious.'

Haroun shrugged and put his headphones back on. 'Play the conversation again and I'll prove it to you,' he said.

*

💜 Our matchmaking software has matched you with *Agahan*. *Agahan* lives in your area and like you she is interested in *camels* and *chemistry*.

💜 *Zabri*, you have thirty seconds to chat with *Agahan*. Don't be shy!

Zabri:	*Salam aleykum.* Camel saddle sword and song.
Agahan:	*Aleykum asalam.* Today?
Zabri:	Rice blanket sword. Hehe, I'm having trouble imagining you as a woman.
Agahan:	I've just been talking to Soda.
Zabri:	Did he agree to increase the tribute?
Agahan:	Yes. Expect double tomorrow night.
Zabri:	How is the bidding?
Agahan:	No bids yet.
Zabri:	The Baker keeps asking for the Golden Ode of Zuhair.
Agahan:	Give it to him.
Zabri:	*Salam aleykum.*
Agahan:	*Aleykum asalam.*

💜 Your time is up!!! 💜

We hope you enjoyed your speed-date with *Agahan*.

Would you be interested in getting to know *Agahan* better? <u>YES</u> I **NO** **NO**

We are sorry that your date with *Agahan* did not work out. Would you like to try a date with someone else?

<u>YES</u> I <u>NO</u> **YES**

is Soda.'

re,' said Haroun. 'Did you hear it?'

Remy, pressing stop. 'For the fifth

g,' said Haroun, 'far away in the background. *La illaha illa Allah*. There is no God but God.'

'If so, it could be any mosque in the world.'

'Not any mosque. Only the Wahhabist group chants that tune.'

Remy pressed play.

'Salam aleykum.'

'Aleykum asalam. Are you passing the evening in peace, monsieur?'

'Peace only. How do you like your new job?'

'There!' Haroun raised his hand. 'Did you hear that? Two rings, one far away and one closer.'

Remy shook his head. 'I heard a clang of some sort, but it was very faint. It could be anything.'

'The far away ring was a mechanic in the next street, banging a tyre off its rim to get at the inner tube.'

'And the closer one?'

'The ring of hammer on anvil.'

'A silversmith, you said?'

'Yes. A silversmith uses a delicate hammer so the pitch is high. A blacksmith's hammer makes a deeper, fuller ring.'

Remy looked at Haroun in wonder.

Haroun smiled. 'When you herd cows in the bush,' he said, 'silence becomes your friend. You notice little sounds.'

'When this is over,' laughed Remy, 'I'm taking you back to France to work in CAL, our Communications Analysis Laboratory.'

Remy fast-forwarded the conversation between Hamsetu and her co-wife and arrived at the moment when Fifi returned to her master's shoulder.

'Soda, do we have a deal or not?'

'Yes, monsieur, we have a deal.'

'There's the chanting again,' said Haroun. 'Do you hear it?'

Remy shook his head.

'Alors – Salam aleykum.'

'Aleykum asalam.'

'Just there,' said Haroun, 'before he puts the phone down, a clicking sound like a grey woodpecker.'

Remy frowned. 'A woodpecker in a silversmith's workshop?'

'I said *like* a woodpecker. I don't know what it is.'

'Glad to hear there's something you don't know,' said Remy. 'I was beginning to think I had a djinn in my library.'

They took their headphones off and Remy poured two cups of strong coffee from a flask.

'Merci,' said Haroun.

'De rien. Do you know where that silversmith works?'

'Yes. There is only one Wahhabist prayer house in Tinzar, and that's in sector 5. There is a mechanic's workshop a couple streets west of there. In between the prayer house and the mechanic's is a silver-shop.'

'Who owns the shop?'

'Anoot and Mustafa Anil. They are *inhadan*.'

'*Inhadan?*'

'Tuareg craftsmen.'

Remy slid a keyboard out from underneath his work-surface and typed *Anoot Anil* and *Mustafa Anil*.

Haroun stared at Remy's fingers on the keyboard. 'That's it,' he said.

'What?'

'The grey woodpecker.'

A computer keyboard. Remy looked at Haroun and wagged his finger appreciatively at him. 'You're the best agent I've ever had.'

'I'm not your agent.' Haroun stood up and made for the door. 'I am only helping you because I want to know the truth about Tinzar.'

'Wait!' called Remy. 'Let me drive you home.'

The door clicked shut. The boy had already left.

6

When Haroun arrived at the mine the next day, he went straight to the Maintenance Department. His supervisor Rahiim was there, his wrinkly feet poking out from underneath a Uranico truck.

'*Salam aleykum*,' said Haroun and began to load light bulbs into his trolley.

Rahiim slid out from underneath the truck on a wheeled tray. '*Aleykum asalam*,' he said. 'You're needed at the acid plant. Someone just called to report a broken bulb.'

The sulphuric acid plant was in the far corner of the mining compound – a large industrial unit of vast vats and snaking steel pipes. Sulphuric acid was an important ingredient in the treatment of uranium ore. Until last year the mine used to bring sulphuric acid in from outside, but now they made their acid on site.

'I thought the acid plant only operated in the mornings,' said Haroun. 'Have they changed the schedule?'

'Ask them when you get there,' said Rahiim, sliding back under the truck.

Haroun did as he was told. He pushed his trolley through the mining compound, marvelling at the gigantic scale of the machinery. He passed the conveyor belts where uranium rock came up out of the mine. The rock climbed to a great height and then fell down into the Crusher, an enormous cylinder where the uranium was pounded into tiny pieces like millet in a mortar.

Gerard had explained the whole process to him and a group of other workers on his first day at the mine. He had shown them how the tiny pieces of uranium ore passed from the Crusher into a vat of strong sulphuric acid and completely dissolved. Then other chemicals were added – Haroun had forgotten what – and the mixture was dried by gigantic hot-air blowers.

Haroun watched the treated uranium rushing out of the wide exit-pipe of the Drier, a bright yellow powder slithering down into one barrel after another. *Yellow powder.* He stopped dead in his tracks. *What is it they called the finished product? Le yellowcake!*

He felt dizzy. The yellow tribute of Gerard's dying message was not gold at all. It was uranium powder. The mine was paying tribute in yellowcake, the product it was producing. Rahiim had told him many times about the early years of the Uranico mine, the raids carried out by Tuareg rebels, the miners who had been killed and the vehicles which had been stolen. And then the raids suddenly stopped, without anyone knowing the reason for the truce. Now he knew: *Someone in the mine had started paying a yellowcake tribute!*

Haroun had said nothing to Remy about his conversation with Burayma or his success in cracking the Tifinagh code. Knowledge was precious and he still did not fully trust the *tuubaaku*. But this new discovery oppressed him, weighed him down with every step. He must go and tell the Frenchman as soon as possible – as soon as he had replaced this bulb.

When Haroun arrived at the acid plant the acrid smell of sulphur filled his nostrils and made him feel sick. He had only ever been here of a morning, when there had been huge scoop trucks shunting mountains of sulphur from place to place and mine-workers swarming over the acid vat like ants on a watermelon. But now there was no one here. The scoop trucks were parked up, the pumps were silent, the ladders and walkways around the acid vat stood bare and white in the afternoon sun like the ribcage of a dead cow in the desert.

'*Ko ko!*' called Haroun, and his voice bounced to and fro amongst the tangled steel pipes. 'I have brought your light bulb!'

'*Merci,*' said a soft voice behind him. Haroun turned. The man who had spoken wore a hard hat and the bottom half of his face was covered by a white turban.

'My name is Alu,' said the man, his dark eyes twinkling. 'Excuse the turban. They're not strictly allowed but we all wear them here – it's the smell, you know.'

'Yes,' said Haroun, wrinkling his nose. He would have done the same if he worked here. Perhaps the underground galleries were not so bad after all.

'There is a control booth up on the bridge,' said Alu. 'The booth is lit by one 60-watt bulb, but the bulb has burned out.'

Up on the bridge. Haroun's mouth became suddenly dry. 'We Fulani have a proverb,' he said. *'To weli ciiwel welaa huutooru.'*

Alu nodded sympathetically. 'The place which suits the sparrow does not suit the lizard. You are scared of heights. So was I when I started here.'

Haroun was surprised. 'You understand Fulani?'

'A little.' The man's mouth was covered by his turban but his eyes were smiling. 'Just take it one rung at a time, son. Since you're so scared, I will come up there with you.'

'I'm not scared,' said Haroun. He picked two 60-watt bulbs out of his trolley, just in case one was a dud. Then he went over to the ladder attached to the side of the central acid vat. Alu followed him.

Haroun climbed up. His palms were damp with sweat and they kept slipping on the smooth steel rungs. The vat was higher than a *chilluki* tree, higher than a baobab even. *Why does Alu not do the job himself? How many miners does it take to change a light bulb? There is something not right about this.*

'Nice climbing, son,' said Alu, right behind him. 'And nice boots. They're not Uranico boots, are they?'

'No,' said Haroun. 'They were a gift.'

He arrived at the top of the ladder, and stepped sideways onto a steel walkway which led all the way around the rim of the acid vat.

'Look down into the tank,' said Alu, stepping onto the walkway. 'It looks just like water, doesn't it?'

Haroun peered over the rim of the vat at the clear, still liquid below. The sulphurous smell was overpowering.

'Give me that bulb,' said the man.

Haroun handed it to him, then looked around in bewilderment. 'Where is the control booth, Alu?'

'There isn't one,' said the man. 'And please don't call me Alu. It's not my name.'

Haroun froze. *What the—*

'Watch,' said the man, and he tossed the light bulb into the vat. It bobbed for a moment on the surface, then it began to hiss quietly and the glass shattered. Haroun watched in horror as the light bulb dissolved before his eyes.

'Strong stuff,' said the masked man, then as quick as a cobra he struck. Haroun felt a strong hand on the collar of his overalls and he was being heaved over the rim of the vat. The man transferred his grip to Haroun's ankles and lowered him until he was dangling no more than a metre above the surface of the deadly liquid. The bitter sulphur fumes burned his nostrils and stung his eyes.

'A Fulani man is governed by a strict code of honour called *pulaaku*,' said the man in a schoolteachery voice. 'Whatever happens to him, he retains his dignity and reserve. He is not affected by hunger or thirst or grief. He feels no fear and he feels no pain. Isn't that right, Haroun?'

Haroun said nothing. If he shouted for help now, it would be the last sound he would ever make.

'I asked you a question, Fulani! I said, *Isn't that right?*'

'Yes!' Haroun thought about his family's cows one by one in order to suppress his terror. *Naaye, Baleeri, Mallewe, Wuneewe . . .*

'*Dow walanaa faamburu*,' said the man. 'What is up high is not for the frog. That's another of your precious proverbs, is it not?'

'Yes.'

'A frog knows its place,' said the man. 'It has no business with the things beyond its reach.'

'Uh-huh.' *Eere, Saaye, Terkaaye . . .*

'What do you know about tribute?'

'Nothing!' shouted Haroun.

'I think you do,' said the man, and he let go of one leg. Haroun's helmet fell off and he watched with horror as it blistered and dissolved in the acid.

'Timbuktu!' cried Haroun. 'The citizens of Timbuktu used to pay tribute to their imajaghan rulers. They gave a proportion of all the wealth that passed through the city, in return for protection.'

'What about today?' said the man. 'Does Timbuktu still pay tribute to the *imajaghan*?'

'No,' said Haroun. 'Tribute is ancient history.'

Amare, Jamalle, Oole and Huroy. Haroun waited to see if he would live or die.

'That's right, son. Tribute is history. Who gave you these shiny new boots?'

'My uncle Dawda bought them for me in Agadez.'

Haroun felt himself being hauled back to safety and he sat down heavily on the metal walkway. He was alive.

'That was a warning,' said the man, standing over him. 'Now you will go to the director's office and you will hand in your notice. You and your whole family will leave Tinzar by the end of the week. Do you understand?'

Haroun nodded.

'Forget Tinzar, forget the mine, but do not forget me. Wherever you go, I will be with you. Breathe a word to anyone about the tribute, and I will do to you and your cows what I did to Claude Gerard. Do you understand?'

Haroun felt a dull rage building within him and his fingers closed on the spare light bulb in his pocket. He could smash it on the walkway and use the jagged glass as a . . . no, he couldn't.

Up here on the bridge he was helpless, and his attacker knew it full well. *Dow walanaa faamburu.* What is up high is not for a frog.

Haroun nodded again. 'I understand,' he said. The man walked to the ladder and started to climb down. Haroun watched his attacker disappear and noticed that the sleeves of his Uranico uniform were too short for him. Then he looked down at his own hands. Try as he might he could not stop them shaking.

*

'*Entrez!*'

Haroun entered the director's office and found Soda doing press-ups in the middle of the floor. Fifi was sitting on his back enjoying the ride.

'*Salam aleykum,*' said Haroun.

'Thirty-four, thirty-five, thirty-six, what do you want?'

'I want to resign.'

'Thirty-seven, thirty- *what?*'

Very good, thought Haroun. That almost seemed like genuine surprise.

'I have had enough,' he said. 'I am leaving Tinzar.'

'Thirty-eight, thirty-nine, how dare you!' Soda curled his lip in contempt. 'Last year you turned up at this mine with a *fake* birth certificate, *begging* for a job, and against our better judgement we gave you one. And now you stroll in here as cool as a watermelon and say that you have *had enough.* I call that very rude.'

72

Haroun looked at the director. *Was he play-acting? Surely he had given the order to frighten Haroun away?*

'I am resigning for personal reasons,' said Haroun, glancing up at the strip light above his head. 'I want to spend more time with my cows.'

'Very well,' said Soda. 'Come back at ten o'clock tomorrow morning to return your Uranico helmet and overalls. After that I don't want to see you ever again. I will fill your position with someone loyal and hard-working, and you can be sure it won't be a Fulani. Forty, forty-one, forty-two, forty-three . . .'

Haroun left the office and walked to the main gate of the mine. Lieutenant Tamboura met him there and took his radiation card. Tamboura was the head of security at the Uranico mine and was renowned for his efficiency and ruthlessness.

Once outside the gates Haroun wanted to run, but he told himself that the danger had passed. If the man who called himself Alu wanted to kill him, he would have done so. He had probably decided that two suspicious deaths in one week would attract too much attention. There would be a lengthy police investigation. Sensitive operations would be endangered. Secrets would come out.

Haroun had not been bluffing when he said he was going to leave Tinzar. Mining was not honourable work for a Fulani, and neither was spying. The very name Tinzar would always be like a bad odour in his nostrils: the acrid, sulphurous stench of near death.

What do you know about tribute? The masked man had asked the same question that Haroun had asked his friend Burayma only yesterday. Could it be that Burayma was involved in this horrible business? How else could his attacker have found out about his interest in tribute?

Haroun saw a cloud of dust far in front of him and heard the engine of a large vehicle. Then he saw the *Bibliothèque Nomadique* tearing along the road towards him, crashing over potholes and slewing through drifts of sand. He had never seen the library move so fast. Not a single book would be left on the shelves.

The van screeched to a halt alongside him and Remy reached over to open the passenger door. The engine was still running.

'Get in!' shouted the Frenchman.

'No,' said Haroun. 'Weren't you listening to the bug in Soda's office? I quit.'

'Get in,' said Remy. 'We need to talk.'

'No. It's over.'

'Get in,' said Remy, pointing a revolver at Haroun.

Haroun got in. Remy put the weapon back in his inside pocket, did a neat three-point turn and sped off towards Tinzar.

'Sorry to do that to you,' said Remy. 'I had no choice. If you think you can just walk away from all this, you're wrong.'

Haroun said nothing. Fear was giving way to anger.

'What do you know about tribute?' asked Remy.

Not again.

'Nothing,' said Haroun. 'I know nothing.'

'I think you do,' said Remy. 'Why else would they threaten you like that?'

Threaten me like what? Soda did not threaten me. And how could Remy possibly know what happened at the acid plant?

Unless he is one of them.

Haroun opened the passenger door and tried to jump out but the Frenchman grabbed him round the neck and stamped on the brake; the heavy vehicle went into a skid and slewed off the road into a sandbank. The spy's head hit the steering wheel and he momentarily loosened his grip on Haroun.

Haroun lunged out and staggered away from the vehicle. *Remy is one of the yellowcake plotters. They killed Gerard and now they have Soda under continuous surveillance lest he try to tell anyone about the tribute. And they used me to plant the bugs.*

He looked wildly around him. The sand stretched levelly away in every direction except towards the south where there were dunes. He broke into a run.

'Wait!' Remy clambered out of the driver's side, blood trickling from a gash in his forehead. 'It's not what you think.'

Haroun knew that if he could get to the dunes, he had a chance. The Frenchman was armed but he could not shoot someone he couldn't see.

'*Arrêtez,*' cried Remy, running after him. 'Don't be a fool. We're on the same side.'

Haroun ran up the closest dune and slithered down the other side. Keeping low to the ground, he crept around the edge of the next dune, and the next. As children he and Hamma had often tracked each other among sand dunes as a game. Now it was for real.

'Look at your left boot!' Remy's voice was fainter now. 'Under the tongue.'

Left boot? Haroun put another dune in between him and his pursuer, then bent down and peered under the tongue of his left boot. *Surely not.* He whipped the boot off, loosened the laces and pulled the tongue right back. A tiny black button adhered to the black leather tongue. *So that's how Remy knew about the acid plant. He gave me the boots so that he could bug his own agent! Whenever I am within fifty metres of Soda's car, the tuubaaku can hear everything I say.*

'Please don't be angry,' called Remy. 'That bug is for your own safety.'

'It hasn't helped me much so far, has it?' shouted Haroun. 'It didn't stop me being dangled over a vat of acid.'

'I'm sorry about that. I came as fast as I could.'

'Leave me alone, *Tuubaaku.*' Haroun could feel tears pricking his eyes and he fought them back. He had not cried in six years, not since that day at primary school when Naabo Normé had stolen his couscous and given it to a donkey. He looked down at his hands, which had started shaking again.

Remy appeared at the top of the dune and

slithered ungracefully down the slope towards Haroun. 'I can't leave you alone,' he said, sitting down next to him. 'You know too much.'

Man and boy sat side by side on the sand, leaning back against the dune and watching the vultures circling above them.

'How is your head?' asked Haroun at last.

'It hurts,' said Remy. 'Tell me about the tribute.'

Haroun hesitated. *Breathe a word to anyone about the tribute, and I will do to you and your cows what I did to Claude Gerard.*

'He threatened my cows,' said Haroun.

'I know,' said Remy. 'He will live to regret doing that. Tell me about the tribute.'

Haroun took a deep breath and began to talk. He told Remy about the Tuareg rebels stopping their attacks on the mine. About the meaning of Gerard's Tifinagh message. The tribute being paid in yellowcake. The masked man desperate to protect the secret.

When Haroun finished his story a strange relief crept over him. The truth had been passed on; let the *tuubaaku* do with it what he liked. He stood up and began to brush the sand off his trousers.

'Haroun,' said Remy, looking up at him. 'Don't quit now.'

'We Fulani have a proverb,' said Haroun. '*Mbuuku bumdo nde wootere yaabete.* A blind man's testicles are only trodden on once.'

'What is that supposed to mean?'

'What happened to me today at the acid plant was not nice. I'm not letting it happen again.'

The Frenchman nodded. A muscle twitched in his jaw.

'What?' said Haroun. 'What are you looking like that for?'

Remy sighed. 'Do you know what would happen, Haroun, if a small nuclear bomb went off in Tinzar?'

'It would blow up the town.'

'Correct,' said Remy. 'It would blow all of Tinzar as high as heaven. There would be a release of heat so fierce that it charred the skin of everyone within eight miles and a flash of light so bright that it blinded everyone within *twenty* miles.'

'*Zorki*,' said Haroun.

'Then the blast wave – a wall of death travelling at hundreds of miles an hour – every hut from Agadez to Aridal would burst open like a kernel of popcorn. Firestorms would rage across the province of Shinn, burning up trees, cows, people and anything else combustible.'

'Why are you telling—'

'Then the nuclear fallout. All the dirt and sand which had been swept up into the explosion would fall out of the sky over four hundred square miles of desert. Black rain, they call it. Five out of every ten nomads in the area would die a slow, painful death and the sand under their feet would remain radioactive for seventy years.'

'Okay, okay,' said Haroun. 'Why are you telling me this?'

'Because that's what would happen if yellowcake got into the wrong hands. This thing is bigger than your testicles, Haroun. It involves hundreds of thousands of people.'

Haroun shook his head. 'You can't make a bomb with yellowcake. Gerard told us that when he gave us our tour of the mine.'

'That's technically true,' said Remy. 'Set fire to a barrel of yellowcake and nothing happens. But if you take that barrel of yellowcake and enrich it, you end up with little coins of uranium 235, each of which contains enough neutrons to blow up five thousand cows.'

Haroun stared at him. 'You're making this up,' he said.

'Okay, I made up the five thousand cows thing. But the rest is true, I swear. Don't let anyone tell you that yellowcake is harmless. It's not.'

Haroun picked up a handful of sand and let it trickle through his fingers. He was wishing his parents had never come to Tinzar. Of all the places where cattle could graze, they had certainly chosen the most frightening.

'I don't see why you still want my help,' said Haroun. 'Go to the police. Play them the tape from the shoe bug.'

'They wouldn't be interested. If the tribute stops, then the raids start again, and that's the last thing the police want. Do you know how many policemen died in Niger during the Tuareg Rebellion?'

'No.'

'Hundreds,' said Remy. 'Including more than a hundred in the Battle of Tchin-Tchabaradin Police Station.'

Haroun clicked deep down in his throat. 'I see,' he said. 'No police, then.'

'No police,' said Remy. 'Just you and me.'

Haroun shook his head. 'Actually, just you.'

7

BIDMARKT 🕐

You are logged in as **Bitesize**.
Item number 330029056051:
Useless Rubbish (15kg of coins)

Starting bid:	**€45,500,000.00**
End time:	**1 day 2 hours 10 mins**
Item location:	**Niger**
Item condition:	**New**
Payment options:	**Cash or bearer bonds**
Delivery options:	**Pick-up only**

Ask seller a question:

From:	**Bitesize**
To:	**Agahan**
Item:	**Useless Rubbish (15kg of coins)**

Greetings. I am the leader of a group of freedom-seekers called Bayt Saïz. I need some Useless Rubbish to put into a Box of Miscellaneous Bits. Are your coins more than 90% Useless Rubbish 235?

*

81

Dusk was falling in the bush outside Tinzar.

'Brother!' cried Haroun. He was at the back of the herd chivvying slackers with twirls of his staff. 'Did you hear Amadou talking about Mahadaga last night?'

Hamma was at the front of the herd, letting out high-pitched whistles as he led the cows down to the river to drink. 'Grass as high as your waist? Mango trees aplenty? Rivers so deep you can't stand up in them? I heard him.'

Hamma pulled a catapult out of his pocket, fitted a stone, took aim and fired. A sparrow dropped out of the sky.

'Let's go there,' said Haroun.

Hamma picked up the dead sparrow and put it in his pocket. 'We don't need to go to Mahadaga,' he said. 'There is plenty of grass right here.'

Haroun arrived next to his brother and squatted on his haunches, watching the cows drink. The sun was setting behind the *chilluki* trees in the west, silhouetting the thorny branches against a blaze of orange.

Haroun tried again. 'Did you hear what Amadou said about the Mahadaga girls?'

'Don't start on that,' laughed Hamma. 'Yes, I heard him. Indigo dresses, pale skin, tattooed lips and gold earrings the size of cola nuts.'

'Well?'

'God gives the rains for us to fatten our

cows,' said Hamma, 'not to chase after indigo dresses.'

Might as well tell him, thought Haroun. 'A man at the mine today told me that if we don't move away from Tinzar, he will shoot our cows.'

Hamma wobbled and put his right leg down. 'Did you steal money from him?'

'No.'

'Are you sure? Think hard.'

'I did not steal anything from him.'

'Right.' Hamma sounded doubtful. 'Justice is on your side, then. We stay.'

The cows drank until their thirst was quenched and then turned and headed for home. Haroun and Hamma followed them side by side, their staffs across the back of their shoulders. For the second time that day, Haroun recounted the whole story, starting with Gerard's death and ending with the yellowcake threat. His brother listened without a flicker of expression.

'So you see,' said Haroun, 'we have to go to Mahadaga.'

Hamma fished a cola nut out of his pocket and took a bite. 'What does the *tuubaaku* say? Does he want you to go to Mahadaga?'

Haroun wondered whether to lie and decided not to. 'He wants me to stay,' he said slowly. 'He seems to think I can help him.'

'And you don't want to?'

Haroun tutted loudly and threw his staff at

Terkaaye, who was veering away from the rest of the herd. She trotted back into line. 'You've never been dangled over a lake of flesh-eating water,' said Haroun, 'or you wouldn't ask me that.'

Hamma spat orange cola juice on the ground. 'Better to be eaten up by water than by self-pity. You're already dissolving, brother. A few minutes more and I won't recognise you.'

'You agree with the *tuubaaku*?'

'Of course. He cannot succeed on his own. *Kodo e wuro, kam remata parnga*. It is the guest in the village whose crops fail. *Tuubaaku* has courage and clever gadgets but he doesn't know the land.'

'He won't give up,' said Haroun.

'Then he will get himself killed,' said Hamma. 'Don't look so sad, brother. You'll be in Mahadaga by that time, goggling at mango trees and tattooed lips.'

Haroun felt his nostrils twitch in fury. 'I'm not thinking about mango trees, Yellowteeth, I'm thinking about our cows. If we stay, they get shot.'

Hamma grinned and waved his staff in Haroun's face. 'Leave the cows to me. If anyone comes within a hundred yards of them with a rifle, I will beat him with this until he can't tell a cow from a cucumber. And if you don't go and help that *tuubaaku* of yours this minute, I'll do the same to you.'

*

BIDMARKT ⊘

From:	Agahan
To:	Bitesize
Re:	item number 330029056051

Thank you for your interest in our Useless Rubbish 235 coins. Our Baker has achieved 92% Useless Rubbish 235, which we trust will be suitable for your Box of Miscellaneous Bits. Blessings on your bid.

*

'How short do you want it?'

'As short as it was on the day of my naming ceremony.'

The young *coiffeur* shrugged and removed the attachment on his clippers.

Road-side night barbers were common in Tinzar because a set of clippers and a paraffin lamp were all that were needed to start up in business. The boy cutting Haroun's hair was new in town and grateful for any clients he could get. He set to work enthusiastically with clippers and razor blade.

'Don't forget the reeds by the lake,' said Haroun.

'*Quoi?*' The barber was not used to Fulani riddles.

'Eyebrows. Shave my eyebrows.'

'Completely?'

'Yes.'

The eyebrows came off. 'Even your own mother won't recognise you,' chortled the barber.

It's not my mother I'm worried about, thought Haroun. *It's masked men with guns.* He gave the barber a 100-franc coin and headed for sector 5. A wizened marabout was begging outside the Wahhabist prayer house, collecting alms in a battered prayer hat.

'*Salam aleykum, Abba,*' said Haroun.

'*Aleykum asalam.*'

'Give me your prayer hat,' said Haroun, 'and I will give you this turban.'

'How long is it?'

'Four metres.'

The marabout tipped his earnings onto the ground, handed Haroun the prayer hat and took the turban.

'Why do you want that old thing?' said the old man, but his benefactor was no longer there.

*

● http://contact.bidmarkt.fr/askquestion&id=330029056051

BIDMARKT ⊙

You are logged in as **Natsqaret**

Item number 330029056051:

Useless Rubbish (15kg of coins)

| Current bid: | €45,500,000.00 (<u>Bitesize</u>) |
| End time: | **22 hours 10 minutes** |

Ask seller a question:

From:	**Natsqaret**
To:	**Agahan**
Item:	Useless Rubbish (15kg of coins)

Salam aleykum. Warm greetings from the People's Republic of Teraqstan, of which I am Minister for Self-Defence. I have two questions:

1. Will you be selling more useless rubbish in the future? We are looking for a regular and reliable source.
2. Would you consider setting a *Buy it Now* price for your useless rubbish? It is unseemly for a Minister of Self-Defence to participate in the last-minute scramble of a bidmarkt auction.

*

The *Bibliothèque Nomadique* was parked outside Mecca Mechanics, its front bumper dented and its bonnet propped open. A muscle-bound Zerma man bent over the engine while his young apprentice held a torch for him.

Haroun took off his prayer hat and approached the library. *'Allah hokku chellal!'* he sang out. May God give you health.

'Get away from there,' said the mechanic. 'How can he give you alms, if he isn't even inside?'

Haroun backed away and crouched down in the dust, hanging his head in shame. A piteous figure he seemed.

'I said get away from there,' snarled the mechanic.

Haroun was scanning the ground on the driver's side of the vehicle and he suddenly saw what he was looking for. He sighed heavily, put on his hat and began to walk away, his eyes still fixed on the ground. Not until he was out of sight of the mechanic did he quicken his pace. It was just as he feared. The footprints of Remy's sandals were headed straight for the Anil brothers' workshop.

Anoot and Mustafa Anil were known in Tinzar for their finesse in handling delicate filaments of silver. They were also known for their finesse in handling bar brawls. Haroun hoped the Frenchman knew what he was doing.

Four doors away from the silver shop, Haroun stopped and took off his prayer hat.

'*Allah hokku chellal!*' he sang out.

'May God provide!' came a voice from within.

Haroun moved on to the next door.

'*Allah winndu baraaje!*' May God write blessings.

The door opened and a crust of bread was placed in his outstretched hand. Haroun ate the bread and moved on to the next door.

'*Allah hokku chellal!*'

'May God provide!' cried a voice within.

The door of the silversmith opened and a man stepped out into the street. The bulk of his turban and the sword hanging from the belt of his robes showed that this was no craftsman. The man glanced at Haroun, then with a graceful swish of his robes he turned and stalked away down the dark street.

Haroun stepped up to the door of the silver shop. *Bijouterie Moderne* read the sign above the door. He lingered, listening to the tap of a silver hammer within and the occasional puff of bellows.

'C'est combien, ce croix-là?'

Haroun recognised the voice. Remy was alive.

'Douze mille.' The voice which replied was gruff and guttural, one of the Anil brothers.

'Je te fais cinq mille.' So the Frenchman was bargaining for jewellery, was he? Probably wanting to plant some sort of bug, and hoping that something would distract the silversmiths' attention. *Here goes.*

'Allah hokku chellal!' sang Haroun.

'May God provide!' replied the gruff voice within.

'Allah winndu baraaje!' sang Haroun.

'I said, may God provide!'

Haroun waited a few seconds and then at the top of his voice he sang out, *'Allah hokku jam!'* May God give peace!

The door swung open and there stood Anoot Anil brandishing his silver-hammer. Behind him Mustafa and Remy sat cross-legged on a Persian rug, a dazzling assortment of silver rings and silver necklaces and silver bangles spread out between them. A teapot hissed on a charcoal stove. A computer idled in the corner.

The silversmith's hammer descended on

Haroun's forehead, a quick, sharp blow which made him reel.

'May God provide,' growled Anoot.

Perfect, thought Haroun. He staggered and fell forward over the threshold of the workshop.

Silence.

'That's a Wahhabist disciple!' said Mustafa in Tamasheq. 'You've killed a Wahhabist disciple!'

Haroun's Tamasheq was far from fluent but during the course of his friendship with Burayma he had picked up the basics.

'I can't have killed him,' said Anoot. 'I hardly touched him.'

'Give him a poke.'

A sandalled toe prodded Haroun in the stomach. Then he felt himself being dragged into the street by his ankles.

'You can't do that to a Wahhabist disciple,' said Mustafa. 'Don't you fear God?'

'He'll be fine here. He'll come round.'

'What if he doesn't? The Teacher will be coming back any minute. Do you want him to find a dead Wahhabist on the doorstep?'

'He's not dead. Look, he's moving.'

Haroun opened his eyes and saw the Anil brothers standing over him. He blinked rapidly and smiled. '*Salam aleykum*,' he said. 'Where am I?'

'Nowhere,' muttered Anoot, but he sounded relieved rather than angry. The brothers went back into the workshop and shut the door firmly behind them.

Haroun walked back along the street towards

Mecca Mechanics. He stopped and crouched in the shadow of a low mud-brick wall, within sight of the door of *Bijouterie Moderne*. The Tuareg noble returned and entered the shop, and a few minutes later Remy came out, carrying a black plastic bag.

'Buy anything?' said Haroun as the Frenchman passed him.

Remy jumped. 'Who's there?'

Haroun stepped out of the shadows. 'Plant anything?'

'You are *formidable*,' said Remy. 'Where are your eyebrows?'

'I lost them.'

'How is your head?'

'Hurts,' said Haroun. 'I hope you bought me something nice.'

Remy looked up and down the deserted street. 'I did,' he said, reaching into the black carrier bag. 'This!' He pulled out a gleaming silver dagger.

*

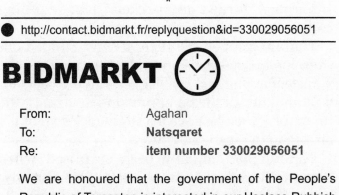

http://contact.bidmarkt.fr/replyquestion&id=330029056051

BIDMARKT

From:	Agahan
To:	**Natsqaret**
Re:	**item number 330029056051**

We are honoured that the government of the People's Republic of Teraqstan is interested in our Useless Rubbish 235. Here are answers to your questions:

1. We will soon be in a position to supply you with a constant flow of Useless Rubbish.
2. We will consider a *Buy it Now* option next time.

Blessings on your bid.

*

At Mecca Mechanics the work on the *Bibliothèque Nomadique* was finished. The mechanic and his apprentice sat on a bench passing a bowl of millet beer to and fro between them. Haroun lurked behind a large pile of tyres and watched.

He saw Remy approach and shake hands with the two men. He saw them go over to the library, open the bonnet and peer inside. The barrel-chested mechanic began to explain to the Frenchman the work he had done, shaking his head and making expansive *kaput* gestures.

The two men began the centuries-old charade of negotiation, complete with jovial back-slapping, forlorn head-shaking, shoulder-shrugging, turned-out pockets, bloodcurdling oaths and incredulous laughs.

Haroun gripped the silver dagger, slipped out from his hiding-place and rolled underneath the vehicle. He plunged the dagger into the back left tyre until he felt the point pressing up against the inner tube, then he gave it a slight nick so that the air began to escape slowly.

Haroun had initially been surprised when Remy told him to slash the van's tyres. But now he understood. Back at the *Bijouterie*, while he had been playing dead, Remy had managed to clip a Keysnatcher onto the back of the Anils' computer. This tiny gadget would record every key press and would transmit it to a remote receiver in the library van. So it was essential that the van pass the night within one hundred metres of the Keysnatcher. What better excuse than slashed tyres? A van being repaired at Mecca Mechanics could hardly arouse suspicion.

Haroun punctured the back right tyre and then crawled forward towards the front of the van. He was now so close to the bargaining men that he could smell their feet, as well as hear clearly what they were saying.

'*Wallaahi Allah*,' said the mechanic. 'Thirty-two thousand does not even cover the price of the parts, let alone the labour.'

'Come, my friend, we both know the price of those parts. They're not even originals. I can see from here that the timer belt is Chinese.'

'*Wallaahi*, it is not Chinese.' The mechanic stamped his foot, filling Haroun's nostrils with dust. 'Look there, MADE IN JAPAN.'

'That says MAD IN JAPAN,' cried Remy, 'and it's written on in biro!'

Haroun plunged his knife into the front left tyre, and Remy must have heard the hiss because he suddenly raised his voice in a torrent of French expletives.

'*Calmez-vous, Monsieur!*' The mechanic was clearly shocked. 'The voice of a chief is quiet, *Monsieur.*'

Haroun stabbed the last tyre. The air pressure

in the tyre was too high and the air rushed out with a loud, agonising hiss.

'*Serpent!*' cried Remy, and the three sets of feet leapt away from the vehicle. The mechanic peered under the chassis and his lips curled back into a vicious snarl.

'*You!*'

'*Salam aleykum,*' said Haroun. He rolled out sideways from underneath the library and scrambled to his feet. The mechanic was coming at him but the millet beer had made his reactions slow. Haroun ducked under his arms and backed up against the pile of tyres he had been hiding behind just a few moments ago.

There was no way out. The mechanic and his apprentice were now on either side of him, advancing towards him with their arms stretched wide as if trying to trap an unruly hen.

Haroun scrambled backwards up the mountain of tyres, until he was crouching right on top. He looked up at the corrugated iron roof of the Mecca Mechanics awning and measured the distance, trying to imagine the roof as the branch of a *chilluki* tree. Out herding in the bush he had often made similar jumps in order to shake down *chilluki* pods for the cows. But never quite this high. And never with so much at stake.

The furious mechanic cursed and began to clamber up the tyres towards him. Haroun jumped. He caught the edge of the corrugated iron, adjusted his grip and pulled himself up onto the roof.

'*Vite, vite!*' The mechanic was gesturing to his apprentice. 'Get round the back! Don't let him get away!' Haroun crept quickly across the roof, and climbed down the other side.

'TAXI!' he yelled. Taxi-motorbikes were common in Tinzar and Haroun could see one parked a little way down the street. The motorbike pulled up alongside Haroun. The rider looked about sixteen and he wore a Bob Marley T-shirt and a multicoloured Rasta beret. If he was surprised to see a Wahhabist disciple clamber off a roof and call for a taxi, he did not show it.

'Where to?'

'Sector 4,' said Haroun.

'A thousand francs.'

Haroun shook his head. 'Two hundred.'

The mechanic's apprentice emerged from a side street twenty or thirty metres back and sprinted towards them.

'Eight hundred francs,' said the Rasta.

'Five hundred,' said Haroun, glancing nervously at his pursuer. 'Deal or no deal?'

The biker took a pair of sunglasses out of his top pocket and put them on. 'Deal,' he said, stamping down on the kick-start. Haroun got on and they roared away down the street.

'Why is that boy chasing you?' asked the Rasta, looking in his rear-view mirror.

'He just won five hundred francs off me in a game of *Aztec*.'

'And?'

'I don't have five hundred francs.'

'Oh. Okay.'

The bike roared through the narrow streets of Tinzar, kicking up clouds of dust on either side. Haroun glanced back over his shoulder. His pursuer was nowhere to be seen.

'I don't get it,' shouted the Rasta over the noise of the engine. 'If you don't have five hundred francs, how are you going to pay *me*?'

'I'm going to give you a silver dagger,' shouted Haroun. 'It's worth much more than five hundred.'

'Oh. Okay.'

They rode on. Haroun looked at the blur of mud-brick walls and houses rushing past on either side, and for the first time that night he began to relax. The evening's work was well done. The Keysnatcher would transmit a record of every key pressed on the Anils' computer. It would be midday tomorrow by the time Mecca Mechanics got those punctures fixed, so the *Bibliothèque Nomadique* would be within range of the Keysnatcher signal all night and all morning. Whatever that computer was being used for, Remy and Haroun would soon know about it.

'I still don't get it,' shouted the moto-boy. 'Why didn't you give *him* the dagger?'

'Who?' shouted Haroun.

'That lad you owed money to.'

'I forgot I had it with me!'

'Oh,' said the Rasta. 'Okay.'

8

ROOM 101
CHATCHATCHAT ☕

Please enter your username: Agahan
Please enter your password: tiwse

There is [1] person in **Room 101**.
Enter? **YES** I <u>NO</u> **YES**

Welcome to Room 101, *Agahan*. *Zabri* is here.

Zabri:	***Salam aleykum.***
Agahan:	*Aleykum asalam.* Fifty years ago what did the imajaghan desire?
Zabri:	**Camelsaddleswordsong.**
Agahan:	And today?
Zabri:	**Riceblanketsword.**
Agahan:	Bids are starting to come in.

97

Zabri:	**Who is bidding?**
Agahan:	Bayt Saïz and Teraqstan.
Zabri:	**How long is left?**
Agahan:	Just under 20 hours. How are things there?
Zabri:	**The baking is very slow.**
Agahan:	Silva is very slow.
Zabri:	**The Baker says his hours are too long.**
Agahan:	Give him the Golden Ode of Imru-Ul-Quais.
Zabri:	**When is the next consignment of yellowcake?**
Agahan:	Tomorrow.
Zabri:	**When tomorrow?**
Agahan:	Leaves the mine at 8pm. Salam aleykum.
Zabri:	***Aleykum asalam.***

***Agahan** has left the room.*

*

Haroun woke to find that the sun had risen. Judging by the tracks in the sand, Hamma and the cows had set off quite recently, heading north towards the salt-lick at Mondé-So.

Haroun washed and prayed, then rolled up his straw sleeping mat and took it into his hut. He saw Hamma's indigo turban lying on the ground, and put it on. Then he stuffed his Uranico uniform and his old boots into a goatskin bag, slung it over his shoulder and went back outside. The time had come to pay his friend Burayma a visit.

Burayma lived on the edge of Tinzar with his parents and grandparents and brothers and sisters and uncles and aunts and cousins.

Hospitality was a strong point of the *imajaghan* and Haroun always enjoyed his visits to Burayma's family. In the ag Ahmed tent the leather cushions were plump, the tea was sweet and the dates were soft.

As Haroun approached, he saw Burayma outside the wall of the family compound, laying a rug across the saddle of a kneeling camel. When he saw Haroun his eyes widened.

'Get out of here!' said Burayma. So much for *imajaghan* hospitality.

'*Salam aley—*'

'I said get *out* of here. On second thoughts, get on the camel. It's quicker.'

Haroun climbed up into the saddle and Burayma got on behind him. The camel unfurled its various knees, stood up, and stalked down the slope towards Tinzar.

'Where are your eyebrows?' said Burayma.

'I lost them.'

'Why weren't you at work yesterday?'

'I resigned.'

'Why?'

'Because someone dangled me over a vat of sulphuric acid and told me to.'

'*Subahaanalaahi.*'

'He also told me to leave Tinzar by the end of the week.'

'That's today, Haroun.' Burayma tugged his sleeve. 'Why haven't you left?'

'Because a wise man once said that we nomads are like sand; we cannot be held in the palm of the hand. If we always do what we are told we are no better than—'

'That was not a wise man, Haroun, that was me. Ignore what I said and leave Tinzar as soon as you can.'

They were on level sand now, walking through a desert slum of corrugated iron shelters. The stale odour of camel wafted into Haroun's nostrils.

'When I asked you about tribute,' whispered Haroun, 'who did you tell?'

'No one,' said Burayma.

'Good.' Haroun tugged at the reins of the camel to turn it around. 'In that case, let's go back to your family tent and talk there.'

'Give the reins to me,' said Burayma. 'We cannot go back there.'

But Haroun did not hand over the reins. The camel began to trot back up the sandy slope and Burayma's family compound came into view over the brow of the hill.

'I wonder who I'll meet in your family tent,' said Haroun. 'Is your father there today? What about your uncles?'

The camel neared the gate of the compound. Burayma's little sister Ramatu stood at the gate, holding a kitten in each hand.

'If he sees you here, he'll kill you,' said Burayma. 'The acid vat was a warning. He will not warn you again.'

'*Who?*' said Haroun.

'My uncle.'

'Which uncle?'

'Abdullai baa Samba.'

'Thank you,' said Haroun. '*Now* we can go.' He pulled the camel's reins across to one side and kicked its flank hard. There was nothing he wanted less than to meet Uncle Abdullai again.

The camel refused to budge. It stood there at the gate, snorting and braying in furious protest. The little girl squealed and hugged the kittens to her chest.

'Help!' she screamed. 'Aghlam is possessed!'

'Shut up, Ramatu!' shouted Burayma. 'You're frightening her.'

Haroun heard voices and footsteps, family members hurrying to see the mad camel.

'Aghlam is possessed by djinns!' sobbed Ramatu.

'Cover your face,' hissed Burayma. Haroun did not need to be told; he was already pulling the lower half of the indigo turban up over his mouth and nose.

Burayma's father came to the wall of the compound, doing his best to arrange his affable face into a frown. 'This is a shameful display, son,' he said. 'Control her.'

Burayma slid down off the saddle and ran around to the front of the camel. Aghlam lunged at him with bared teeth but Burayma dodged nimbly aside and grabbed her nose. As he tightened his grip on Aghlam's sensitive nostrils, she quickly realised who was boss.

'Good boy, Bura,' said a soft voice. 'We'll make an *imajaghan* of you yet.'

Haroun recognised the voice immediately and he could almost smell the sulphuric acid. There in the gateway stood Haroun's attacker, his robes and turban dazzlingly white in the midday sun.

'Won't you introduce us to your guest, Bura? Come and join us, friend, for a glass of bitter tea.'

'*Merci*,' croaked Haroun, reaching up to make the eye-slot in his turban even narrower.

'We have to go, Uncle.' Burayma was back in the saddle, clicking his tongue against his teeth to make the camel rise.

'No.' Abdullai walked forward and took hold of Aghlam's reins. 'I will not let it be said that a guest came to the ag Ahmed tent and left without having drunk so much as a cup of water.'

'Let them go, brother,' chuckled Burayma's father. 'Camels can be harnessed but boys can not. Let them seek adventure while they may.'

Abdullai reluctantly handed the reins back to Burayma. He was gazing at Haroun intently, as if trying to see through the folds of the boy's turban.

'Aghlam is very tall, is she not?' he said. 'Are you afraid of heights, guest?'

Burayma kicked Aghlam's flank and she began to walk off down the slope.

'*Dow walanaa faamburu!*' called Abdullai. 'What is up high is not for a frog.'

Haroun looked at him sharply; he could not help it. A flash of recognition passed between them.

'Wait!' cried Abdullai. 'Stop that camel!'

'I can't!' called Burayma, as Aghlam trotted off across the deep sand.

Abdullai watched them dip out of sight below the crest of the dune. Then he turned to his niece who was still standing at his side nuzzling her kittens.

'Ramatu,' he said. 'Bring me my rifle.'

The little girl beamed. 'Are you going hunting, Uncle Abdullai?'

'Yes.'

'What are you going to kill, Uncle?'

Abdullai's dark eyes twinkled playfully. 'This and that,' he said.

*

Blaise Soda arrived at work in a bad mood. He stopped his car at the front gate of the mining zone and wound down the window. Lieutenant Tamboura came out of his booth and approached the car.

'*Bonjour, Monsieur Directeur,*' said Tamboura. He wore a peaked cap and a khaki version of the Uranico uniform.

'*Un très bon jour,*' said Soda. '*Un très bon jour* for *Monsieur Directeur* to FIRE YOU.'

The lieutenant stepped back a pace. 'Something wrong?' he asked.

Soda picked a black plastic box off the

103

passenger seat and waved it under the guard's nose. 'What do you think this is? Go on, take a guess.'

'*Je ne sais pas, Monsieur.*'

'I'll tell you what it is, you lacklustre louse of a lieutenant. It's an amplifier for a radio-microphone. And it has run my car battery down so far that the engine refused to start this morning.'

'Why was there an amplifier on your – *OUCH!*'

'*Pardon-moi,*' said Soda. 'My hand slipped. Why, you ask, was there an amplifier on my car battery? I have not the faintest idea. But you will give me an answer to that question within forty-five minutes, or else I will drop all security personnel into the Crusher. And you, Lieutenant, will be first.'

Soda left his startled head of security at the gate and drove to the Administration Block. He got out, opened the bonnet of his car and carefully clipped the amplifier back onto the battery. *Whoever has done this thing,* thought Soda, *they must not know I am on to them.*

*

'What is your Uncle Abdullai up to, Burayma?'

Haroun and Burayma were walking through the streets of Tinzar on Aghlam's back.

'He doesn't tell me,' said Burayma. 'I have not yet come of age, remember?'

Haroun nodded. He remembered when Burayma's elder brother Amadou had come of age at sixteen. Amadou's uncles and cousins had attacked him with a ceremonial turban and wound it tightly around his eyes and mouth. That was Amadou's first turban and he wore it to this day.

'Uncle Abdullai doesn't talk to me directly,' continued Burayma, 'but I overhear things. A comment here. A whisper there. Enough to get suspicious.'

'*Nowru walaa omboode,*' murmured Haroun. 'An ear does not have a lid.'

'My uncle thinks the glory days are coming back,' said Burayma. 'He talks about Timbuktu, Tchin-Tchabaradin and Tinzar in the same breath.'

'Tchin-Tchabaradin was hardly a glory day,' said Haroun. 'The government fought back, didn't they? They killed thousands of *imajaghan* men, women and children.'

'He talks about that, too,' said Burayma. 'The government is made up of ignorant farmers, he says. They hate us nomads and do everything they can to wipe us out. But *we* are the rightful rulers of the land. It is in the nature of the *imajaghan* to rule.'

'Right.' Haroun was beginning to get the picture. Uncle Abdullai was both arrogant and angry.

'He gets his ideas from the Teacher,' said Burayma. 'The Teacher is a great chief who travels around the country, rallying the *imajaghan*. This year he seems to have settled in Tinzar.'

The Teacher. Haroun remembered the *imajaghan* at the *Bijouterie Moderne*: the bulk of the turban, the curve of the sword, the graceful swish of fine waxed robes.

'Does the Teacher want to restart the rebellion?' asked Haroun.

Burayma paused before answering. 'He's doing *something*, but I don't know what. That day in the tunnel, when you asked me about tribute, you scared me.'

'And you went and told your uncle about it?'

Burayma nodded miserably. 'He said he wanted to meet you. He borrowed my Uranico uniform and ID to get him into the mine.'

Haroun remembered that the sleeves of his attacker's uniform had been too short for him. It was beginning to make sense.

'Burayma, your uncle is involved in something terrible,' said Haroun. 'I will need your help to stop him.'

'You're asking me to betray my own family,' said Burayma.

'I'm asking you to do what's right.'

'I don't know what's right, and neither do you,' snapped Burayma. 'When I come of age, I'll be free to choose my own way. But for now, I sleep in my family's compound, I eat their rice and I respect their ways.'

Haroun did not answer. He unwound his turban until all four metres of the indigo fabric lay loose across his palms.

Burayma frowned. 'Why have you taken off your—'

Haroun spun round in the saddle and

punched Burayma on the jaw. Then he brought the indigo turban down behind his friend's neck. 'Congratulations,' he said, winding it across Burayma's chin. 'It's time to come of age.'

Burayma grabbed Haroun's wrists. 'You can't do that,' he said. 'I'm not even sixteen.'

'Of course you are,' said Haroun, winding the turban around his friend's head. 'I've seen your birth certificate.'

'You know I faked that certificate. You helped me do it, you globule of gecko spit.' Burayma jumped down to the ground and began to run.

Haroun stood up in Aghlam's saddle and leapt down on top of the fleeing Tuareg, slamming him face first into the sand. He pulled Burayma's left arm up behind his back and wound the turban across his mouth.

'Here are the rules of manhood,' said Haroun. 'Drink water to be handsome. Fill up with sun to be strong. Gaze at the sky to be great.'

'Get off me!' Burayma's voice was muffled.

'Now you are a man,' said Haroun. 'Start talking like one.'

'Boil your head!'

Haroun tied the loose end of the turban around Aghlam's back leg and knotted it firmly. Then he stood up and walked off.

'I need your help,' said Haroun over his shoulder. 'Come to my settlement tonight and we will talk.'

'Never!' cried Burayma. 'This is the last time we talk in this life or the next.'

Haroun looked up at the sun. It was almost time for the Tahala rendezvous with Remy and he was aching to find out what secrets the Keysnatcher had revealed. But there was something he must do first. He must go to the mine one last time and hand in his Uranico overalls and boots.

9

Spurred on by the prospect of being dropped into the Crusher, Lieutenant Tamboura worked quickly and efficiently. He swept the Administration Block for bugs and then hurried off to find Soda.

He found him down in the mine, supervising the dynamite slotting at Face A. Today was a Deaf Day so more chunks of uranium ore would be blown out of the ground.

Lieutenant Tamboura approached Soda and cleared his throat loudly. 'I have found a bug,' he said.

Soda turned round and his helmet lamp flashed full into the lieutenant's face. 'Where?'

'The electric light in your office. It was in the casing.'

'Let me see it.'

The lieutenant held out the palm of his hand. 'It's tiny,' he said. 'Probably military spec. If an amplifier is nearby, this thing can transmit several kilometres.'

'Is it transmitting what we are saying now?'

'Here in the mine?' The lieutenant shook his head. 'Impossible.'

The miners had finished slotting the dynamite and they crept back along the tunnel to where Soda and Tamboura stood. One of them set a detonator down on the ground, knelt behind it and began to count down. *Dix, neuf, huit, sept . . .*

'What shall I do with the bug?' asked Lieutenant Tamboura.

Six, cinq, quatre . . .

'Put it back exactly where you found it.'

Trois, deux . . .

'Monsieur?'

Un.

'Put . . . it . . . back.'

Zero.

An ear-pummelling boom sounded through the galleries, and a white flash illuminated Blaise Soda's face for a second: his mouth was a thin, hard line and there was rage behind his eyes.

Soda had no doubt about who had planted that bug. In due course the culprit would be punished severely, but for now he must suspect nothing. The bug must continue transmitting as normal.

'Listen, Lieutenant.' Soda's usually shrill voice was low and measured. 'That Fulani boy who resigned yesterday will come to the mine today to drop off his Uranico uniform. You will let me know the moment he arrives.'

'Oui, Monsieur Directeur.'

*

Abdullai baa Samba stood in Tinzar market place and looked around. He spotted a group of milkmaids sitting underneath a wooden shelter at the far end of the market. Fulani girls were recognisable by their rich blue dresses and the large silver coins plaited into their hair. Abdullai hid his rifle in a cluster of parked bicycles and approached the girls.

'*Jam weeti*,' he said to one of them. 'Are you passing the morning in peace?'

The Fulani looked up from her calabash of milk. She had a small tattoo on her cheek and a pretty gap between her front teeth. 'Peace only,' she replied. 'And you?'

'Peace only. I am looking for a boy called Haroun. He used to work at the Uranico mine.'

The coins in the girl's hair clinked as she nodded. 'Diallo Haroun,' she said. 'He lives with his parents by the Tombutu baobab tree west of Tinzar.'

'May God reward you,' said Abdullai. He turned on his heel and walked away into the bustle of the market. Millet grain, peanuts, prayer hats, prayer mats, watch repairs, turbans, aspirin, Thai rice, tamarind, Coca-Cola, cooking pots, biros, coconuts, sunglasses, batteries, breadfruit – Abdullai baa Samba ignored it all. He retrieved his rifle from amongst the bicycles and headed west.

*

Lieutenant Tamboura lounged in his security booth and looked out over the mining compound. Everything was working perfectly: the Exit Belt was belching uranium ore out of the ground and passing it on to the Crusher, the Chemical Vat and the Drier. Five colossal sixteen-wheelers were parked by the Drier. By tomorrow evening those lorries would be hundreds of miles away in Benin, loading their yellowcake onto ships bound for France. Except for one, of course, which would be unloaded much sooner. Tonight was tribute night.

'*Salam aleykum*, Lieutenant.'

The sudden voice at his elbow made the security man start. He took his feet off the desk and turned to face the newcomer. It was the Fulani boy who had resigned the previous day, the one whose arrival Soda had asked him to report.

'*Aleykum asalam*,' said Tamboura. 'Don't creep up on me like that.'

The Fulani boy took a goatskin bag off his shoulder and emptied its contents on the desk. Blue Uranico overalls and a pair of battered boots.

Tamboura picked up the boots with his left hand and made a show of examining them. With his right hand he took his phone from his pocket and held it under the desk, tapping out a short text message:

FULANI IS HERE

FIND NAME IN ADDRESS BOOK.

'Can I go now?' said the boy.

'No,' said Tamboura. 'You have not given me your helmet yet.'

SEND MESSAGE?
YES
SENDING ...

'It fell into a well,' said Haroun.

'How unfortunate,' said the lieutenant. 'We will have to take the cost of the helmet out of your pay.'

'How much does that leave me with?'

'Let me see.' The security man pretended to do sums in his head. 'That leaves you with nothing.'

The boy's crestfallen expression was delightful. That would teach him to plant bugs in the director's office.

Tamboura's phone vibrated in his hand, and he coughed to disguise the sound. A text was coming through.

'Look at those lorries,' said the lieutenant. 'Beautiful beasts, aren't they?'

The Fulani boy looked towards the convoy and Tamboura glanced down at his phone.

READ MESSAGE?
YES

LET THE PUP GO.
HE WILL LEAD
US TO BIG DOG.

Tamboura was disappointed. This Fulani boy was the reason Soda had threatened to drop him and his security department into the Crusher. But the director's logic was correct. This Fulani was just an agent. If followed, he would lead them to the real enemy.

'Get out of here,' said Tamboura. 'From this moment, you are no longer welcome at Uranico.'

*

Abdullai baa Samba hid his rifle in the hollow of the Tombutu baobab tree and approached the door of one of the two Fulani huts.

'*Ko, ko,*' he called, clapping his hands quietly. '*Salam aleykum.*'

'*Aleykum asalam,*' came a male voice within. 'Are you passing the day in peace?'

'Peace only,' murmured Abdullai, peering into the darkness and pressing his right hand to his heart in a gesture of respect. 'It is Haroun I am looking for.'

'I have not seen my son since daybreak,' said the voice from the darkness. 'He would usually be on his way to the mine at this time, but he lost his job there.'

'Perhaps he is herding,' suggested Abdullai.

'Perhaps.'

Abdullai's eyes adjusted to the gloom and he saw a traditional Fulani four-poster bed. On top of the bed were laid at least twenty millet stalk mats, and on top of the mats lay a middle-aged man with a short goatee beard and a black shepherding cloak.

'Where does he take the cows?'

'The salt-lick at Mondé So. Who are you?'

'My name is Jibliiru,' said Abdullai. 'Give my greetings to Haroun.'

'He will hear.'

'*Salam aleykum.*'

'*Aleykum asalam.*'

Abdullai retrieved his rifle from the hollow of the baobab tree and set off north towards Mondé So. He had told the boy to leave town and the boy had not listened. Now the boy must die.

*

When the sun was high in the sky, Haroun arrived at the mining village of Tahala and made his way to the rendezvous point. The *Bibliothèque Nomadique* was there, looking strangely small amongst the lone and level sands.

'*Oss, oss,*' cried Haroun as he approached the library. He opened one of the back doors and climbed in.

'*Fermez la porte,*' said Remy. The bookshelves had been pulled back and the Frenchman was sitting staring at the computer screen, his chin resting on one hand. Haroun closed the door.

'*Stop, oh my friend,*' said Remy. '*Let us pause to weep over my beloved Unaizah. Here was her tent on the edge of the sandy desert between Dakhool and Howmal.*'

'*Aleykum asalam,*' said Haroun. 'What are you talking about?'

'It's the beginning of a poem,' said Remy, swivelling round in his chair. The bags under his eyes and dishevelled hair suggested a sleepless night.

'What poem?'

'The Golden Ode of Imru-Ul-Quais. One of six poems stolen from the Jeddah Museum in Saudi Arabia a few days ago.'

'Who would bother stealing a poem?'

'Who indeed!' Remy swivelled back to face the computer and pressed a key. A block of writing appeared on the screen:

```
<PWRON> http://www.chatchatchat.com <ENTER>
Agahan <TAB> tiwse <ENTER> Y <ENTER>
Aleykum asalam. Fifty years ago, what did the
imajaghan desire? <ENTER> And today? <ENTER>
Bids are starting to come in. <ENTER> Bayt Saïz
and Teraqstan. <ENTER> Just under 20 hours. How
are things there? <ENTER> Silva is very slow.
<ENTER> Give him the Golden Ode of Imru-Ul-
Quais. <ENTER> Tomorrow <ENTER> Leaves the
mine at 8pm. Salam aleykum. <ENTER> <ESC>
```

Haroun read the text three times but it made no sense at all.

'That was typed on the keyboard in the *Bijouterie*,' said Remy. 'The Keysnatcher transmitted it late last night, after you left. Very impressive getaway, by the way.'

'*Merci.*'

'The text was typed on a chat site by someone calling himself Agahan. Do you know anyone of that name?'

Haroun shook his head, wondering what a chat site was.

'False name, probably,' said Remy. 'The only person I saw using the computer last night was that *imajaghan* with the classy robes. He must use the *Bijouterie* as a communications base.'

Haroun read the text again, but it was still no clearer to him. There were too many words he did not understand.

'The problem with the Keysnatcher,' continued Remy, 'is that you can only see half of the conversation – the half being typed on the bugged keyboard – and for the other half you have to use your imagination. What we have here is a rendezvous in an obscure internet chatroom. Agahan enters his username and password and goes into Room 101, where person or persons unknown are waiting for him. The first question looks like a security question, confirming the identity of whoever is there. Then he starts talking about bidding. Ever heard of Bayt Saïz?'

'No,' said Haroun, whose head was hurting.

'Nasty little terrorist group in North Africa. And Teraqstan is a nasty little dictatorship in

Central Asia. Whatever these people are bidding for, it's not coffee.'

'Yellowcake,' said Haroun.

'That's what I'm afraid of,' said Remy. 'Then we come to Silva. *Silva is very slow.* Who is Silva and what does he do very slowly?'

'No idea,' said Haroun.

'Maybe he means da Silva. Are there any South Americans in Tinzar?'

'No.'

'Thought not,' said Remy. 'Then there's our friend Imru-Ul-Quais. The person on the other side of that conversation has the Golden Ode of Imru-Ul-Quais and is going to give it to Silva.'

Haroun was beginning to feel stupid – a rare and unpleasant sensation. 'How do you know that Imru-Ul-Quais is a poem?' he asked. 'How do you know it was stolen?'

Remy grinned. 'The same way I know about Bayt Saïz and Teraqstan,' he said. 'This computer is connected to the internet via a satellite phone.'

Haroun frowned. Any more of this nonsense and he would leave the *tuubaaku* and go back to his cows. The place which suits the sparrow does not suit the lizard.

'I'll explain another time,' said Remy. 'Suffice to say that I asked my computer what it knows about Imru-Ul-Quais and it told me.'

'Fine.' Haroun shrugged. 'So why not ask it what it knows about Silva?'

'I'll show you why not,' said Remy, his fingers pecking at the keyboard. 'The name is far too common. There, you see, it knows *too much* about Silva, 104,000,000 pages worth. That's far too many to even begin to—*égua!*'

'What is it?' asked Haroun.

Remy was leaning in towards the computer, flicking from one page of dense text to another.

'What?' said Haroun.

'*Je suis idiot*,' said Remy. 'S-I-L-V-A!'

*

By the time Abdullai Baa Samba arrived at Mondé So, it was almost time for afternoon prayer. He crouched in the shade of a *chilluki* tree, took a small pouch of gunpowder out of his top pocket and gazed at the idyllic scene before him.

There were about ten cows grazing contentedly in the clearing before him, lowering their heads to lick the salt-rich earth and then lifting them to emit loud drawn-out sighs of satisfaction. A boy stood among the cows, balancing on one leg like a stork. Abdullai could tell the boy was Fulani by the way he held his staff across the back of his shoulders. Abdullai poured gunpowder into the rifle's chamber and tamped it down. Then he raised the rifle to his shoulder and aligned the sights.

'*Salam aleykum*, Haroun,' he mouthed, putting his finger on the trigger. 'Your meddling days are over.'

The target turned slightly and Abdullai saw him side-on. *Subahaanalaahi. It's not him.*

The Fulani boy ducked out of the viewfinder

of the rifle and Abdullai lowered his gun. The boy was crouching on the ground, raising a cola nut to his mouth. No, he was fitting it to a catapult. He was taking aim.

Abdullai baa Samba brought the rifle back up to his shoulder a moment too late. The cola nut hit him between the eyes and he blacked out.

10

Haroun leaned over the Frenchman's shoulder and gazed at the blur of words falling upwards like reverse rain.

'S-I-L-V-A,' whispered Remy. *'Séparation Isotopique par Laser sur Vapeur Atomique.* Here in Africa? Surely not!'

'What's wrong?' said Haroun.

'The *imajaghan* have got hold of a Laser Isotope Separator. They are enriching yellowcake.'

'C'est grave?'

Remy unplugged the satellite phone and dialled a number. His face had turned even whiter than its normal *tuubaaku* colour. *'C'est une catastrophe,'* he said. 'If the *imajaghan* have succeeded in enriching yellowcake, then they have in their hands the Holy Grail: undeclared unmonitored weapons-grade uranium.'

'Zorki,' said Haroun. 'The wall of death. They're selling it to the highest bidder.'

Remy was talking on the phone. 'This is Pigeon,' he said, 'I have intercepted a message from Tuareg rebels here in Tinzar. It mentions *Séparation Isotopique* . . . No, we do not have photos. We do not even know where the laboratory is.'

He put the phone down and leaned back in his chair.

'Who were you talking to?' said Haroun.

'Henri Lupin,' said Remy, 'Commander of the GIGN.'

'What's that?'

'*Groupe Intervention du Gendarmerie Nationale.* They are the French military's elite counter-terrorism unit. I want Lupin to bring his team here.'

'What did he say?'

'He said he would ring us back in two minutes. In the meantime . . .' Remy tapped a couple of keys on the computer and a block of text appeared at the top of the screen:

```
<PWRON>   http://www.saharamail.ne   <ENTER>
Agahan <TAB> tiwse <ENTER> Zabri@saharamail.ne
<TAB>  Re: Meeting <TAB>  Next meeting 21
septembre 10pm @ chessville.fr <ENTER>
```

'*Voilà!*' said Remy. 'What do you make of that?'

'It looks like another of last night's Keysnatcher transmissions,' said Haroun.

'Very good. It came through at about midnight. Looks like Agahan has been emailing his man Zabri, arranging their next chat for 10pm tomorrow night. This message might be useful to us – it gives us the password for Agahan's email account.'

'*Tiwse?*' said Haroun.

'*Exactement.*'

The satellite phone rang and Remy began to talk in such fast French that Haroun hardly understood a word. But he could see from Remy's face that the news was not good.

'*Sacré bleu,*' said Remy, putting the phone back in his pocket.

'Lupin?' asked Haroun.

'Yes. He is going to drop a parachute team onto the Shinn Massif.'

'To take over your mission?'

'No. They cannot act until they have the GPS coordinates of the laboratory and proof that uranium is being enriched there.'

'Why?' said Haroun.

'Politics,' grumbled Remy. 'Niger is no longer a French territory. If we send the troops in and we turn out to be wrong, it will provoke a diplomatic crisis. We have to be a hundred per cent sure.'

'I see,' said Haroun. 'So how are we going to find the SILVA laboratory?'

'Simple,' said Remy. 'We follow the yellowcake convoy, and then we follow the tribute and see where it goes. We know that the convoy leaves the mine at 8pm. That gives us three hours to make a plan.'

Click.

Haroun looked up sharply. *When you herd cows in the bush, silence becomes your friend. You notice little sounds.* He tiptoed across to the back doors of the van and drew the bolts across.

'What is it?' said Remy.

Haroun made a gun shape with his right hand and pointed with his left hand to where the sound had come from. Remy knelt down and drew back a sliding trapdoor in the floor of the van. He stuck his head through the trapdoor and peered out. Whatever he saw, he did not like it. He jumped up, dived into the driver's seat and turned the keys in the ignition.

'Ne quittez pas!' barked a voice outside the back doors. 'This is Lieutenant Tamboura, Uranico head of security. Come out with your hands up.'

Remy revved the engine. The wheels spun, digging the van deeper and deeper into the sand. A shot rang out and the back left tyre collapsed beneath them.

'*Zut,*' said Remy. 'I just had that tyre fixed.'

The door handles at the back of the van jiggled furiously, but the bolts held fast. The Frenchman yanked the four-wheel drive lever towards him and slammed the accelerator pedal all the way to the floor. The engine screamed in protest.

Haroun climbed through into the passenger seat just as Tamboura's face appeared at the driver's window. The barrel of his revolver was up against the glass.

'Turn off the engine,' mouthed Tamboura.

The three remaining tyres got a grip on the ground beneath them and the *Bibliothèque*

Nomadique lurched up out of its rut. Tamboura fired too late, shattering the driver's window but missing Remy.

'Hold on,' said Remy, his knuckles white on the steering wheel. 'It is hard to control this van in sand, and even harder at high speed.'

And even harder with a burst tyre, thought Haroun, as the vehicle slewed from side to side. He heard the revving of motorbike engines far behind them, and a voice barking out commands.

'Dirt bikes,' said Remy. 'They wanted to surprise us so they left their bikes back there and came for us on foot. How did they find us? Is my cover blown?'

'I don't know.'

The library van flew over rock and sand, sliding from side to side on its burst tyre. Haroun glanced in the wing mirrors and saw three motorbikes weaving in and out of view. The situation was hopeless.

'Listen carefully,' said Remy. 'In three minutes or less, those bikes will catch up with us and Uranico security officers will board the van. They will arrest us for breaches of mine security. We will be handed over to the police and locked up.'

Pullo yidaa ombeede, thought Haroun, holding onto his seat. A Fulani hates being imprisoned.

'Unless,' continued Remy, 'we can arrange for you to escape and continue the mission on your own.'

Haroun considered this. Continuing the

mission had to be better than going to prison. He looked in the wing mirror and saw one of the bikers taking aim with a handgun. Three shots sounded and the van's back right tyre exploded beneath them.

'We Fulani have a proverb,' said Haroun. '*Walaa hiraande hadataa jemma warde.* Even if dinner is not ready, night still falls.'

'Meaning?'

'I will continue the mission. I have no choice.'

Remy picked up the sat-phone and dialled.

'This is Pigeon,' he said. 'My cover is blown. Agent H will continue the mission alone.'

The grass was much longer here and Haroun judged that there must be a riverbed nearby. The motorbikes were hot on the van's tail, lions closing in on a wounded wildebeest. Behind the bikes, Haroun saw a white Toyota following at a safe distance. *Blaise Soda.*

Remy handed Haroun a small key. 'There is a compartment in front of your seat there. Open it.'

Haroun opened the compartment and a bundle of wires and gadgets burst out of it like the intestines of a sacrificial sheep.

'You will need those things for your mission,' said Remy. 'The camera and the sat phone you know about already. As for the GPS trackers, the instructions are in there somewhere.'

Haroun shoved the tangled mass of technology into his goatskin bag. '*Wanaa nyaande loongal rawaandu suuwetee,*' he muttered. 'The day of the hunt is not the time to go out and buy a dog.'

A volley of shots raked the undercarriage of the van. Both front tyres burst and the vehicle spun out of control.

'End of the road,' said Remy. 'Get in the back, Haroun. They must not see you.'

There was a dry riverbed in front of them. Travelling on its wheel rims, the *Bibliothèque Nomadique* careered down the bank into the deep sand and began to carve a path through it. The steering wheel twisted this way and that, mimicking the death throes of the axles beneath. In the middle of the riverbed the engine died.

Two of the pursuing motorbikes crossed the riverbed, kicking up a fine spray of sand as they overtook the stranded library. The bikers stopped, removed their helmets and exchanged glances of mingled relief and triumph. Then one of them gave a minuscule nod: time to go in for the kill. They ran forward, leapt onto the bonnet of the library, kicked in what remained of the windscreen and climbed through into the cab.

*

● http://contact.bidmarkt.fr/itemnumber330029056051/detail.psp

BIDMARKT 🕐

You are logged in as **Bitesize**.
Item number 330029056051:
Useless Rubbish (15kg of coins)

127

*

Blaise Soda had enjoyed the chase but he was glad it was over. He got out of his truck and clambered down into the riverbed. The *Bibliothèque* was axle-deep in fine white sand and one of his security men was guarding the back doors.

'Is the Lieutenant inside?' asked Soda.

The guard nodded.

'*Salut*, Lieutenant!' shouted Soda. 'It seems that our librarian's *nomadique* days are over.'

Metal bolts grated and the double doors at the back of the van swung open. The floor of the library was covered with books. There in the middle of the books stood the French librarian. His hands were on his head and sweat glistened on his brow. Tamboura and another guard stood on either side of the Frenchman, pointing their handguns straight at him.

Soda peered into the gloomy interior of the van, taking in the nearly empty shelves and the piles of fallen books.

'Where is he?' said Soda. 'Where is the boy?'

'He is not here,' said Tamboura.

'Not here? Don't be an imbecile, Lieutenant. We both saw him get into the van.'

The Lieutenant shrugged. 'There is a trapdoor here,' he said, kicking a dictionary into the hole to prove it.

Soda shook his head. 'Impossible. We would have seen him, if he had jumped.'

'We passed through some long grass not far back. Perhaps he jumped out there.'

Silence.

'You two,' Soda gestured to the guards. 'Go back to the long grass, find the Fulani boy and bring him here. If in fifteen minutes I do not see him standing in front of me, I will feed your kidneys to my ferret.'

'But, Monsieur, he could be anywhere—'

'*Allez!*'

The two men set off on their Fulani-hunt, leaving Soda and Tamboura to guard Remy.

'Well done, Lieutenant,' said Soda. 'You have run our spy to ground.'

Remy hung his head. 'I am a librarian,' he said. 'I travel around and lend books to children.'

'You mean you travel around and lend *bugs* to children.' Soda's eyes flashed. 'You used one of my own workers to bug my office.'

'I don't know what you are talking about.'

'And you used my own car to hide your infernal amplifier—' Soda broke off, choking on his fury. 'I call that unutterably rude!'

The Frenchman raised his head and looked Soda in the eyes. 'Did you have Gerard killed?' he said.

'*Non*,' said Soda.

'I think you did. I think you killed him because he found out that his workers had been leaking yellowcake to Tuareg rebels. You killed him to protect the secret.'

'Rubbish,' growled Soda. 'The Teacher arranged for one of his own men to kill Gerard. I had nothing to do with it, do you hear?'

'I don't believe you,' said Remy.

Soda pouted. 'I am disappointed,' he said. 'I had expected an intelligent discussion, yet you produce nothing but wild accusations. Africa is complex, library-man. Read some of your books and then maybe we will talk again.'

'Africa is complex,' repeated Remy. 'Is that what I am to tell Gerard's family? That Africa is complex?'

'Yes,' said Soda. 'And while you're at it, tell them that Gerard chose to come here. Tell them he knew the risks. Tell them he had a very pleasant life in Tinzar. Tell them he lived in an air-conditioned house with thick carpets and that he employed a full-time chef. Tell them he earned two hundred times more than an average miner's wage. Tell them whatever you like, you interfering prig.'

*

The bikers crisscrossed back and forth through the long grass, keeping their helmet visors up so as not to restrict their view. They were looking out for a blade of flattened grass, a footprint, anything to suggest that a boy had passed this way.

Nothing.

'Perhaps he is a djinn!' shouted one. 'They say that the Grinning Djinns of Shinn can make themselves invisible.'

'I have heard that too,' shouted the other. 'You can only make them reappear by splashing them with coffee.'

'Which we don't have.'

'Let's go back.'

'Soda said that if we came back empty-handed he would feed our kidneys to his ferret.'

'He won't do that. Tonight we're riding shotgun on his yellowcake convoy.'

'Okay. Let's go back.'

*

'Niger is the poorest country in the world,' said Soda. 'Did you know that, library-man?'

'Yes,' said Remy.

'And two-thirds of Niger's income is from the sale of yellowcake.'

'I know,' said Remy.

'Clever you,' said Soda. 'No doubt you also know that not so long ago we had Tuareg rebels raiding the mine every month. I was the foreman at Uranico. I was responsible for the lives of my men.' Soda fell silent; he did not like even thinking about the years of the Tinzar raids. The police had not wanted to get involved, so he and his men had taken up weapons themselves to defend the mine against the invaders.

'You fought them off?' asked Remy.

'Yes,' said Soda. 'At first it was easy because they had swords and we had rifles.'

'Hardly fair,' agreed Remy.

'But then they got hold of guns. We were miners, not soldiers. We began to suffer heavy casualties.' Soda paused. If he closed his eyes he could still hear the raid sirens and the splutter of Kalashnikovs.

'So you negotiated a truce,' said Remy.

'I had no choice. Two-thirds of Niger's income is from uranium sales and without that uranium our country would collapse. I met with the rebel leaders six months ago.'

'And?'

'They demanded a tribute, a share of the mine's yellowcake. I agreed.'

Remy stepped forward and whispered in Soda's ear, 'The rebels have a Laser Isotope Separator.'

Soda reeled. '*Non,*' he said. '*Ce n'est pas vrai.*'

'*C'est vrai,*' said Remy.

'You are bluffing. There is no way that the *imajaghan* could acquire SILVA, let alone recruit a scientist capable of using it.'

'They have done. I can show you messages we have intercepted—'

'Intelligence can be faked.'

'*Écoutes.*' Remy's voice was strained. 'I know you are angry about the bugs, but try and think clearly. You can help me—'

'Bugs?' said Soda. 'What do you mean, *bugs*? We found only one bug, the one in my office.'

'One bug,' said Remy. 'That's right.'

'*You said bugs.*' Soda's voice was menacing. 'How many are there? Where are the others?'

Curled up in the computer alcove behind the bookshelves, Haroun shook his head. How could Remy have made such a simple blunder? Just when it looked like he was gaining the upper hand.

'I will give you five seconds to tell me where all the bugs are,' said Soda. 'If you do not, Lieutenant Tamboura here will shoot you.'

'There are no more bugs,' said Remy.

'*Cinq,*' said Soda.

'There are no more bugs.'

'*Quatre.*'

'Don't do this, Soda.'

'*Trois.*'

'Please, no.'

'*Deux.*'

Haroun lifted the latch which held the shelves in position and he braced himself to rush to Remy's rescue.

'*Un.*'

'I bugged your ferret's collar,' said Remy.

Silence.

Haroun let the latch fall quietly back into place. *God help you, Remy.*

'Fifi?' Soda sounded horrified. '*Espèce de vache!* Of all the spies in the history of Africa, you will go down as the most despicable.'

'I did what was necessary,' said Remy.

'Did you now?' sneered Soda. 'In that case, I

133

will also do what is necessary. I will make sure that the Tinzar police allocate you their smallest cell and that they keep you as their guest for an unimaginably long time.'

'While imajaghan terrorists walk free?'

'You are not an African, library-man. The *imajaghan* are none of your business. Ah, here are my men.'

The returning guards stammered as they confessed to not having found Haroun. As expected, Soda ranted and raved for several minutes before his anger fizzled out.

'*Monsieur*,' said Lieutenant Tamboura hesitantly. 'You have captured Big Dog. The pup will turn up in due time.'

'He'd better,' said Soda.

'And when he does,' said Tamboura, 'he will join Big Dog, howling in Tinzar prison.'

'Whatever,' Soda muttered. 'Let's get back to the mine.'

Haroun listened to the slam of the library doors, counted three motorbike kick-starts and heard the soft hum of the director's 4x4 moving off. He fumbled with the latch, wrenched the shelves aside and tumbled out of his alcove onto a pile of library books. *Freedom!*

Haroun lay on the floor of the van breathing deeply, with Remy's parting instructions ringing in his ears. *Find the laboratory, get in, take your photos and get out of there.*

11

● http://contact.bidmarkt.fr/itemnumber330029056051/detail.psp

BIDMARKT

You are logged in as Natsqaret.
Item number 330029056051:
Useless Rubbish (15kg of coins)

Your bid:	€77,200,000.00
Previous bids (10)	(Bitesize)
End time:	2 hours 50 minutes

You are currently the highest bidder for this item

*

By the time Haroun knocked at the door of *Cyber Alpha*, the sun was low in the west. *Cyber Alpha* was Tinzar's first and only internet café. The man who opened the door wore a blue corduroy suit and thick-lensed spectacles.

'Are you Alpha?' said Haroun.

Alpha Bari looked at Haroun, taking in the shaved eyebrows, scruffy clothes and goatskin bag. 'Are you lost?'

'No,' said Haroun. 'I need to send an email to my friend Zabri.'

'Do you have an email account?'

'Yes,' said Haroun. 'But I do not use it very often. You will have to help me.'

'One thousand CFA for tuition,' said Alpha, 'and one thousand CFA per hour for the connection.'

'Fine,' said Haroun.

From:	agahan@saharamail.ne
To:	zabri@saharamail.ne
Subject:	Changed meeting

Our next meeting was to have been tomorrow 10pm @ chessville.fr. Things have changed. We must meet tonight. 10pm @ chatchatchat.com

'Very good,' said Alpha. 'Now you simply click SEND. Use the mouse. I already told you. No, that thing with the long tail. That's right. Yes, that's all. Your message is sent.'

*

The sun sank over Tinzar in a blaze of orange, but Haroun did not see it. He was engrossed in the instructions for the GPS receiver, and wishing that he had brought a French dictionary back from the library with him.

Hamma was sitting next to him on the mat and all around them stood the family cows, chewing the cud and flicking their tails to and fro.

'You should have seen me,' said Hamma. 'I felled him with a single cola nut. It was just like one of those kung fu films.'

Haroun turned on one of the trackers and a little red dot began to flash on the screen of the GPS receiver.

'Then I put him on the back of a cow,' said Hamma, 'and took him all the way to that hollow tree at Tin Atoona. It might be hours before he wakes up.'

'What was he wearing?' asked Haroun.

'Robes and turban,' replied Hamma, 'as white as milk.'

Haroun nodded. 'That's Abdullai baa Samba. He killed Claude Gerard.'

'Do you know why?'

'Gerard found out that some Uranico workers were paying a yellowcake tribute to Tuareg rebels. He must have been planning to resign from his position and put a stop to the tribute.'

'I see,' said Hamma. 'The rebels could not let that happen. No more tribute, no more uranium.'

'Exactly. Listen, brother, I need your help.'

'Doing what?'

'Planting these,' said Haroun, holding up the trackers for Hamma to see. 'There are five lorries leaving the mine at 8pm tonight. I need to stop the lorries and stick a tracker on each one. That way we can track the yellowcake wherever it goes.'

'Why does *Tuubaaku* get you to do all the dangerous stuff?' said Hamma. 'Why can't he do something himself for a change?'

'He's been arrested.'

'*Zorki.*' Hamma reached for one of the GPS trackers and inspected it. 'We should stick them on at the mine,' he said, 'before the lorries leave.'

Haroun shook his head. 'The security in the mining compound is too high. It needs to be somewhere on the road outside the mine.'

'Fine,' said Hamma. 'In that case, you make a roadblock of *chilluki* branches just past Tahala. Those branches have thorns as thick as your fingers. The convoy stops, the drivers get out to clear away the thorns, we bug the barrels. Easy.'

The purple sky in the west had faded into grey. The family cows began to stamp their feet in unison, a vain effort to keep mosquitoes at bay. Burayma arrived and plonked himself down on the mat.

'*Salam aleykum,*' said Burayma.

'*Aleykum asalam,*' said Hamma. 'Why are you wearing my turban?'

'Ask Skinkface over there.'

'Burayma came of age this afternoon,' said Haroun. 'Now that he is a man, he wants to help us defeat the rebels.'

Burayma scowled. 'If I help you, will I lose my job at the mine?'

'Only if we get caught,' said Haroun, and he began to explain Hamma's thorn branch plan.

Burayma shook his head. 'A *chilluki* blockade is

too obvious. We might as well leap around yelling YOU ARE BEING HIJACKED!'

'Do you have a better idea?' said Hamma.

Burayma thought. 'Yes. Put a cow on the road.'

Haroun stared. 'A cow?'

'Or five,' said Hamma, shrugging his shoulders.

'Five cows and a camel,' said Burayma. 'Just to be on the safe side.'

Haroun wagged his finger in Burayma's face. 'I do not call that the safe side, you *imaja*-moron. Five lorries, each weighing more than a baobab tree and travelling faster than a cheetah. You think they'll stop for a few cows?'

'They will have to stop. The first driver will be scared of crashing.'

'So we herd our family cows into the path of five juggernauts and then wait and see what happens to them. I'm ashamed of you, brother. You are no longer a Fulani.'

The words stung. Hamma raised his staff high into the air to strike Haroun.

'Don't fight,' said Burayma, moving between them. 'Think about it, Haroun. The cows which run will not get hurt. The cows which don't run will stop the convoy.'

Haroun thought about it. He hated the idea of leading his cows into danger. But what choice did they have?

'Sometimes,' said Burayma, 'a man has to risk the thing he loves the most, in order to overcome the thing he fears the most.'

'I gave you that turban to make you behave like a man,' snarled Haroun. 'Not to make you babble like a djinn.'

*

Siita Sanga turned the key in the ignition and revved. The engine growled throatily, longing to be let loose on the open road.

Sanga had been a driver all his working life. For thirty-five years he had driven mopeds, moto-taxis, bush-taxis, 4x4s, tractors, minibuses and articulated lorries. For the last ten years he had worked for Uranico driving yellowcake lorries from the Tinzar mine to the Benin coast. Tonight he was driving Bead 2, the second lorry in a convoy of five. The convoy was codenamed Yellowstring and Sanga was in charge.

'*Come in, Yellow Leader.*' A gruff voice crackled on the CV radio. '*This is Bead 1. Yellowstring is secure and ready to roll.*'

'I hear you, Bead 1,' said Sanga. '*Allez y.*'

The lead lorry moved off slowly, and Sanga followed suit. In his wing mirror he saw the headlights of Beads 3, 4 and 5. The large double gates of the mining compound were unbolted by unseen hands and drew apart with a loud creak, allowing Yellowstring to drive out into the night.

The lorries were impressive animals – they had sixteen wheels each and were made up of two parts, the 'tractor' in front and the 'trailer' behind. Fully loaded, each one weighed twenty-seven tonnes.

Sanga reached for the radio. *'Shotgun 1, Shotgun 2, this is Yellow Leader.'*

'We hear you, Yellow Leader.'

'Keep your eyes open, both of you. I need you to be extra vigilant tonight.'

'Don't worry, Yellow Leader. The cake is safe with us.'

Siita Sanga did not share the guards' confidence. Two shotguns were hardly a striking display of military might. Yellowstring is vulnerable to attack, thought Sanga. Tuaregs are not the only people with a taste for cake.

The convoy passed Tahala and Tinzar and continued south towards Agadez. The rains of the past months had pitted and scarred the surface of the road and this made for a bone-rattling drive. Sanga gripped the wheel and scowled down at the bumpy dirt road in the arc of his headlights.

Suddenly the lorry in front of Sanga began to sound his horn: a series of short angry blasts. Sanga grabbed the radio:

'Come in, Bead 1.'

The lead lorry did not respond. The short blasts turned into a continuous yowl and the brake lights came on. Sanga took his foot off the accelerator and braked sharply to stop himself crashing into Bead 1's trailer. As he did so he put his left foot on the clutch to break the link between engine and transmission.

'Bead 1!' he shouted. *'What is wrong?'*

There was no reply. The Bead 1 trailer began to

slide sideways. It was going into a rear-wheel skid and in a moment or two it would be completely out of control.

'*Apply the spike, Bead 1!*' The spike was the nickname given to the supplementary trailer brake, an emergency feature designed to bring a skidding lorry under control. But it was already too late. Bead 1's trailer jack-knifed and began to overtake its own tractor, dragging it off the road.

'*Steer into the skid!*' cried Sanga. That was the only thing to be done now – try to keep the vehicle straight by steering in the same direction as the trailer was sliding. As Bead 1 slewed off to the right, Sanga could at last see the obstacle ahead. *Animals*. About thirty metres away stood a huge black bull and behind it were four or five cows. And a dromedary.

Sanga clenched his teeth and his knuckles whitened on the steering wheel. '*Emergency brake, all of you!*' he cried into the radio, his right foot stamping down on the brake pedal. The harsh braking made his wheels lock so he eased off a fraction to unlock them before applying pressure again. It was a technique called cadence braking and it took a lot of practice to get right. Sanga knew that if he locked the brakes for too long, his trailer would go the way of Bead 1 and he would find himself in a terrifying rear-wheel skid.

Sanga's sixteen wheels struggled to grip the surface of the dirt road, propelled towards the animals by the combined momentum of seventeen tonnes of truck and ten tonnes of yellowcake. A small reddish cow turned and bolted off the road. Another followed, and another. They jostled each other in their panic to get away, their eyes rolling and staring. Out of the corner of his eye Sanga thought he saw Bead 1 slide off the road and down onto the grassy verge. Shotgun 1 was still on top of Bead 1's cab, clinging on to its metal frame. *God help him.* In his thirty-five years behind the wheel, Sanga had witnessed several accidents. If a lorry turned over the result was always the same: blood on the road.

Brakes on, brakes off, brakes on, brakes off. Sanga pumped the pedal and gripped the steering wheel tight. He knew the procedure for meeting animals on the road. *Do not swerve to avoid.* If necessary, plough straight through them. *Have lunch*, as his driving instructor used to say. Grisly, of course, but it was the lesser of two evils. Kill a cow or kill yourself.

As the cows scattered, the dromedary also turned and fled. Instead of heading for the grassy verge, the daft animal ran off down the middle of the road – hopped off in fact, for its legs had been tied together with a piece of rope. Muscles rippled in the camel's neck as it strained forward. Sanga sighed with relief as he saw the animals take flight.

He had sighed too soon; the black bull was standing its ground. It turned slowly to face the lorry head on. It lowered its horns and flared its nostrils. It was blinded by the headlights but seemed nevertheless to be looking straight at him. There was fire in its eyes.

Sanga stamped on the brake. He was no longer going fast enough to be in danger of skidding so he put his foot all the way to the floor. *Pedal to the metal,* as his instructor used to say. At the same time he reached forward and yanked the 'spike' lever under the steering wheel column, sensing as he did so the immediate drag of the extra trailer brakes. Fifteen metres. Ten metres. Five. The bull did not even blink. Two metres. One metre. Bead 2 ground to a halt.

Sanga braced. He expected the lorry behind him to plough into the back of his trailer with a sickening crunch, but the impact did not come. *Well done, Bead 3.* He saw Bead 1 over to his right, some way off the road. By good fortune the trailer had not turned over and Shotgun 1 was still on top.

The bull lifted its head slowly and as it did so its horns tapped against the metal framework mounted on the front of the lorry. *Bull bars,* thought Sanga with a sardonic smile. The bull gazed at him through the windscreen of the cab and snorted as if to compliment him on his advanced driving skills. He nodded back to acknowledge the animal's brinkmanship and nerve.

Sanga peered into the darkness beyond the yellow arc of his headlights. There was no one herding these animals, hence the camel's legs being tied. A hobbled camel could not stray far.

He turned off the engine and ran a hand across the stubble on his chin. *A hobbled camel cannot stray far. It is the perfect way to keep an animal in one place.* He grabbed the radio:

'Shotgun 1, Shotgun 2, come in.'

'We hear you, Yellow Leader.'

'Execute Contingency Plan 4.'

Shotgun 2 laughed. *'You need to eat more carrots, Boss. That there is a bull, not a bandit.'*

'Quiet!' Sanga was in no mood for jokes. *'You will treat this situation as a hijack and execute Contingency Plan 4.'*

The years of the Tuareg Rebellion had taught Sanga caution. It was not uncommon to see animals on the road, but there was something too efficient about this bovine roadblock, something almost organised.

Shotgun 1 clambered down off the roof of Bead 1, ran towards the road and fell to one knee in the shadow of a large rock. He paused there, finger on the trigger, scrutinising the area around the convoy for any sign of movement. Sanga leaned out of his window and squinted towards the headlights of Beads 3 to 5. Shotgun 2 was taking up his position across the road from Shotgun 1.

Sanga was not the only person interested in the movements of the security guards. Nearby, Haroun and Burayma were lying on their bellies in the sand, watching the guards deploy.

'This is not good,' whispered Haroun. 'Why would they do that unless they suspected a hijack?'

'Don't worry,' said Burayma. 'We'll get our chance.'

Haroun was less optimistic. 'I told you the cows-on-the-road plan wouldn't work.'

'The lorries have stopped and the cows are alive,' said Burayma. 'You stay here and grumble while I go and help Hamma plant the trackers.' He pulled his turban up over his mouth and started to crawl forward on his stomach.

Haroun had hoped it would not be necessary for Burayma and himself to be directly involved. If Hamma got caught, he would do his 'I'm just a dumb herder' routine. Haroun and Burayma, however, had been Uranico workers for a long time. If they were recognised, difficult questions would be asked.

The lead lorry was stranded off road, its two halves misaligned like a broken bone. Burayma crawled up to the lorry from behind and slipped into the gap between tractor and trailer. He fumbled with the giant hooks which fixed the tarpaulin to the base of the flatbed truck. Then he lifted up the tarpaulin and slipped into the trailer. The security guards did not notice; their eyes were fixed on the road and the other four lorries.

Haroun took out his GPS receiver. In the middle of the screen a red dot appeared, winking conspiratorially at him. *Well done, Burayma.* The first tracker was in place.

Burayma slipped out of the trailer and hooked down the tarpaulin. Then he crawled back to where Haroun lay. 'Something needs to be done about the guards,' he said. 'Hamma can't do his job with those vultures watching.'

'I know,' said Haroun. 'We need something to distract their attention.'

Burayma stood up. 'I'll do it. They won't recognise me in this turban.'

'Get *down*, Burayma,' whispered Haroun, but it was too late. His friend was already strolling towards the road whistling an old *imajaghan* folk song between his teeth.

The security guard behind the rock heard the whistling before he saw Burayma. He lifted the barrel of his Kalashnikov so that it was resting on top of the rock, pointing in the direction of the sound.

'*Qui est-ce?*' he barked.

Burayma walked forward into the beam of Bead 3's headlights, shielding his eyes theatrically against the glare.

'*Agmăyăgh alumin!*' he cried out. Haroun understood the Tamasheq words. *I'm looking for my camel.*

'*Arrêts,*' shouted the guard. 'Stop right there and kneel down.'

'*Aghlam!*' exclaimed Burayma, catching sight of his camel and hurrying towards her.

The two guards ran towards the young Tuareg. As soon as their backs were turned, Haroun crept up onto the road, keeping out of the various headlight beams. He thought he saw a dark figure slip into the gap between the rearmost tractor and trailer. *Go for it, Hamma.*

Burayma knelt down next to Aghlam and started untying the rope around her front legs. He stroked her belly and murmured placatingly. Meanwhile the guards positioned themselves either side of the Bead 2 cab and snarled orders at the young Tuareg.

'Get down on the ground!'

'Move away from the camel!'

'Keep your hands where we can see them!'

Haroun crept up behind the guards and dodged sideways into the gap between the Bead 2 tractor and trailer. He stepped up onto the towbar, grabbed one of the hooks at the base of the tarpaulin and heaved until it came loose. Then he unhooked three more and climbed in.

It was dark inside the lorry and there was hardly any space to move. Haroun could feel barrels, dozens of them, stacked all the way up to the tarpaulin overhead. He took a GPS tracker out of his pocket, and as he did so he heard the door of the cab open and the soft crunch of someone jumping down onto the road.

'He doesn't understand French,' said a man's voice. 'Let me talk to him.'

'He understands,' replied one of the guards sulkily.

'*Salam aleykum, imajaghan,*' said the new voice. '*Ayyu awa tuged, uregh aduruk ammagradagh.*'

Stop what you're doing, I want to talk with you. It was rare for a Zerma to know any Tamasheq and Haroun was impressed.

'*Aleykum asalam.*' Burayma's voice was shaking slightly. 'What do you want with me? I'm just a herder.'

148

'Is this your camel?'

'Yes.'

'Are these your cows?'

'No.'

'Your camel nearly caused a serious accident here.'

'Forgive her. She did not mean any harm.'

Haroun stuck a GPS tracker under the rim of the nearest yellowcake barrel, turned quickly and climbed down onto the towbar.

'Why did you leave her wandering on the road?'

'You know.'

'No, I don't.'

'I had to go.'

'Go?'

'Yes. I feel much better now.'

There was a long silence.

'Take off your turban,' growled Siita Sanga.

12

'You heard me,' said Sanga. 'Take it off.'

'I can't,' stammered Burayma. 'The law of the veil is my guide on the road of sand and stones. The veil hides my face to anger, to pride, to suffering, to love, even to death.'

'What's he on about?' said a guard.

'He doesn't want to take his turban off.'

'The law of the dark veil is lighter than the sun!' cried Burayma, pulling a fold of the turban up over his nose.

Sanga stepped forward and there was a new hardness in his voice. 'Take it off.'

The radio in the driver's cab crackled. *'Yellow Leader, this is Bead 4. Come in, Yellow Leader.'*

Sanga jumped up onto the step of the cab and reached for the radio.

'Come in, Bead 4.'

'Yellow Leader, I can hear someone moving around in my trailer. I think he may be trying to steal cake.'

Sanga moved fast. He gestured for one of the guards to stay with Burayma and for the other one to follow him, then he turned and sprinted towards Bead 4. Perched on the towbar in between the two halves of Sanga's lorry, Haroun shrank back into the shadows and held his breath as the two men rushed past. He looked down at his GPS receiver. Five tiny red markers blinked back at him. *Well done, Hamma,* he thought. *Now get out of there before they find you.* Haroun did not want to imagine what would happen if his brother were caught redhanded in a Uranico cake lorry.

Time to help Burayma escape. Haroun picked a small rock off the road and peered round the side of the lorry. There stood his friend, frozen in the yellow headlights. The guard stood a few paces off, legs apart, rifle pointed casually in the direction of Burayma, a picture of confidence and control. Haroun threw the rock.

As a provocation it worked well. The rock hit the guard on the back of the head. He gave a bellow of outrage and started towards where the rock had come from. Silently Burayma climbed up onto Aghlam's back and moved her towards the front of the lorry. Haroun took hold of the iron rungs on the back of the lorry and climbed swiftly up onto the roof. The guard appeared below him.

'*Salam aleykum,*' whispered Haroun.

The guard looked up with a start and raised his rifle, but Haroun was already off and running. He ran the length of the lorry roof, jumped down on top of the cab, then leapt off onto Aghlam's waiting back. The moment that Haroun landed behind Burayma atop the tufty hump, the camel bolted; she ran off into the desert, bucking and rearing, her riders clinging on for dear life. Haroun looked back to see the guard standing on the roof of the lorry, rifle raised to his shoulder.

'Duck!' he cried.

There was a loud crack and a bullet whizzed over their heads. Aghlam redoubled her speed, falling over herself to get as far as possible from those terrifying juggernauts and angry men.

'What about your brother?' asked Burayma.

Haroun had been wondering the same thing. Hamma had definitely managed to plant the last tracker, and with any luck he had been able to escape before Sanga arrived.

'He's fine,' said Haroun, trying to inject confidence into his voice. 'He'll burrow into the sand and wait until the convoy gets going again. Then he'll round up our family cows and take them home.'

'Okay,' said Burayma. 'Where now?'

'Tinzar,' said Haroun. 'I have an important meeting at *Cyber Alpha*.'

'When?'

Haroun glanced up at the stars. 'About half an hour from now,' he said.

Burayma tweaked Aghlam's reins to turn her nose towards Tinzar. 'Who with?' he asked.

'A close friend of Agahan.'

'You're not serious?' Burayma's eyes were as wide as calabashes.

'Deadly serious,' said Haroun. 'Come along, if you like.'

*

● http://www.chatchatchat.com/room101/javaapplet.js

ROOM 101
CHATCHATCHAT ☕

Haroun stared at the login page in front of him and took a deep breath. He was about to impersonate the Teacher himself, a difficult task and possibly a fatal one.

Please enter your username: Agahan
Please enter your password: tiwse

There are [0] people in Room 101.
Enter? YES I NO YES

Welcome to Room 101, *Agahan*. You are alone.

Agahan: *Salam aleykum.*

No answer. Haroun drummed his fingers on the computer desk. What if Zabri was not coming? What if he suspected a trap?

Burayma was at his side, examining the GPS receiver. 'Convoy still going,' he said.

'You don't need to tell me that every five

seconds,' snapped Haroun. 'Just tell me if it stops, all right?'

When he turned back to his computer screen, he read something which made his heart skip a beat:

Zabri has entered the room.

| Zabri: | *Salam aleykum.* |

Here goes, thought Haroun.

Agahan:	*Aleykum asalam.* Fifty years ago, what did the imajaghan desire?
Zabri:	**Camelsaddleswordandsong.**
Agahan:	And today?
Zabri:	**A pet iguana and an ipod.**

That is not right.

'Hey, Bura,' said Haroun quickly. 'What does the *imajaghan* desire today?'

Burayma looked up from the GPS receiver. 'A plate of rice,' he chuckled, 'a blanket to cover himself and his sword as a souvenir.'

'Where is that from?'

'One of the Agadez poets, I forget who.'

Haroun hesitated. *A pet iguana and an ipod?* Was this some kind of test? Did Zabri suspect that Agahan was not really Agahan?

| Zabri: | **Only joking. A plate of rice, a blanket to cover himself and his sword as a souvenir.** |

Haroun whistled in relief.

154

Agahan:	The questions are important. Take them seriously.
Zabri:	**Sorry.**
Agahan:	Has the tribute arrived?
Zabri:	**Not yet.**
Agahan:	The winners of the auction want photos of the product before they pick up.
Zabri:	**Who won?**

Haroun frowned. He had no idea who had won, or whether the auction was even finished. Who should win? Nasty little terrorist group in North Africa, or nasty little dictatorship in Central Asia?

Let Africa get something for a change.

Agahan:	Bayt Saïz.
Zabri:	**Give me an email address and I will send them photos.**
Agahan:	No. They insist on sending their own photographer – an Algerian boy called Nuuhu.

There was a long pause. Haroun drummed his fingers on his knee. *Swallow the bait. Swallow the bait.*

Zabri:	**When is he coming?**
Agahan:	11pm.
Zabri:	*Subahaanalaahi.* **They work fast.**
Agahan:	They are professionals. Meet the boy at the lab and treat him well. *Salam aleykum.*
Zabri:	*Aleykum asalam.*

You have left Room 101.

Would you like to visit another room? <u>YES</u> I <u>NO</u> **YES**

Haroun leaned back in his chair and puffed out his cheeks. The palms of his hands were sweating.

'Convoy has stopped,' said Burayma.

'Good,' said Haroun. 'They must be offloading the tribute.'

'Let's just hope they offload one of our trackers with it,' said Burayma.

Haroun looked over his shoulder and beckoned to the man in the blue corduroy suit. 'Alpha, can you help me here?'

'What?'

'I need some information.'

Alpha sat down next to Haroun and showed him how to search the net with Google. Together they did practice searches for 'sunglasses' and 'cow medicine' and 'Shinn Massif'. Haroun soon got the hang of it.

'This is incredible,' whispered Burayma when Alpha had gone away. 'See if it's got anything about Mahadaga girls.'

'Shut up and keep your eyes on those trackers,' said Haroun. He glanced over his shoulder and then began to type, stabbing at the keys with one hesitant finger: 'Bayt Saïz'.

The first page which came up was just what Haroun needed:

Bayt Saïz ('House of Saïz') was founded in 2006 by Algerian arms smuggler and mystic Abu Saïz du

156

Hoggar. The group's commanders live in the Hoggar Massif near Tamanrasset and plot the overthrow of the Algerian government. In November 2006 Abu Saïz died and Mustaf Belmustaf du Hoggar became the group's new emir.

'Look at this,' said Burayma, pointing at the screen of the GPS receiver. Haroun looked. Four of the red dots were continuing on their way south towards the coast but one was going north.

'That must be the yellowcake tribute!' said Burayma.

'It looks as if it's coming back to Tinzar,' said Haroun. 'Why the *zorki* are they bringing it back?'

*

● http://contact.bidmarkt.fr/itemnumber330029056051/detail.psp
---

Item number 330029056051:
Useless Rubbish (15kg of coins)

This auction has now ended.

Congratulations, Natsqaret! You have won this item.
Your winning bid was **€92,540,000.00.**

Send seller a message:

Salam aleykum. Warm greetings from the People's Republic of Teraqstan, of which I am Minister for Self-Defence.

It would seem that we have acquired your useless rubbish. Our people in Niamey have chartered a helicopter and are already on their way to pick up the product. They will arrive in two hours or less, so please send us your location (GPS).

If they find the product to be satisfactory, our people will pay €92,000,000 in bearer bonds and €540,000 in cash.

*

'Are you mad?' asked Burayma. 'You can't really be intending to go to that laboratory on your own?'

'I have to go on my own,' said Haroun. 'They are expecting one person and that's what they'll get.'

The boys were standing outside the cybercafé, heatedly discussing their next move. Aghlam knelt in the sand, gazing at the moon from under half-closed eyelids. She seemed blissfully unaware of the argument going on nearby.

'I could wait with Aghlam somewhere out of sight,' said Burayma. 'We'll probably end up having to rescue you again.'

Haroun laughed. 'If I hadn't rescued *you* back there, I wouldn't have needed rescuing myself. Besides, there's something more important I want you to do.'

'What?'

'Go and see if Hamma has arrived home. I'm worried about him.'

'And how are you going to follow the tribute? On foot?'

'I'll borrow a motorbike.'

'Of course you will.' Burayma handed over the GPS receiver and clambered onto Aghlam's hump. '*Salam aleykum.*'

Haroun reached up and shook his hand. '*Aleykum asalam.* Say hello to my brother for me.'

Aghlam stood up and ambled off majestically, carrying Burayma away into the night. Haroun watched them leave, then looked down at the GPS receiver. The yellowcake tribute had almost reached Tahala mining village. There was no time to lose.

I'll borrow a motorbike, he had said. Easier said than done. Haroun did not know anyone who would lend him a bike, and a taxi-moto was out of the question. Algerian terrorists do not travel on the back of taxi-motos, or so he imagined. The only option he could think of was to borrow a taxi-moto and ride it himself. But how to get rid of the driver?

He shuffled down the street, hands in pockets, deep in thought. He had never hijacked a taxi-moto before. He did not want to use a gun or a knife – that would make him as bad as Uncle Abdullai – but what was the alternative? He walked on past the mobile phone kiosk, the baker's oven, the abattoir, the Ahmadiya mosque, the blacksmith's and the poultry market. Then he suddenly stopped and looked back, an idea forming in his mind.

The big poultry merchants had left at sundown, leaving a desultory row of women and children, each clutching a chicken or two, each determined to make a sale even if it took all night. Haroun cast a critical eye over the hens and roosters. None of them looked particularly heroic. He would have to take a chance at random.

A little Zerma girl was squatting at the end of the line with a scrawny speckled hen.

'How much?' said Haroun.

'Seven hundred and fifty francs.'

'Six hundred.'

'Done.' The girl grinned and held out her hand for the money. Now she could go home to bed.

Haroun paid and took the hen, holding it upside down by its legs. It squawked a brief protest and then was silent.

Haroun left the market and hopped over a low brick wall into the Tinzar hospital compound. There were beds all over the moonlit yard, for patients who had not been fortunate enough to get a place inside the building. Some slept, others conversed in low voices with visiting relatives. One man's bed was set up underneath an acacia tree and a drip was suspended from a branch over his head. Malaria.

At the front gate of the hospital, two moto-taxis stood nose to nose, the two riders leaning over their handlebars, trading jokes and insults.

Haroun walked towards them, faking a limp. 'Taxi,' he said.

'*Oui*,' said the two riders in unison.

'Don't choose him,' said one. 'He's new in town. He'll be lost within two minutes, I promise you.'

'Don't choose him,' said the other. 'He'll take you to a dark alleyway and mug you.'

Mugger or New Boy. Great.

Haroun limped up to Mugger, dragging his right leg. 'If you try and mug me,' he said, 'I will set my chicken on you.'

'Where you going?'

'Tahala miners' village.'

'Two thousand francs.'

'Five hundred.'

'No way,' said Mugger. 'It's night, it's a long way and there are two of you.'

'Two of – you are counting my chicken as a passenger?'

'If you would rather leave her with my friend here, I'm sure he would happily look after her.'

New Boy nodded and licked his lips.

'A thousand,' said Haroun wearily.

'Get on,' said Mugger.

Haroun got on and they roared off down the road. Mugger was a wild rider. He was in fifth gear before they were even out of Tinzar, and once on the open road, he really let rip. Haroun watched Mugger's hand and foot movements carefully. It didn't look so hard.

Haroun let go of the hen's legs. With an indignant squawk and a frantic flutter she was gone.

'My hen!' yelled Haroun. 'Hen overboard!'

'Never mind,' said Mugger. 'There wasn't much meat on her anyway.'

'Turn round and let me get her. That hen is half your fare, remember.'

'*Zorki.*' Mugger stamped on the brake pedal and leaned sideways, pulling the bike into a sharp U-turn. He flicked the headlamp onto full beam and accelerated back down the road the way he had come.

'There she is!' cried Haroun. His speckled hen was legging it down the road in front of them, enjoying sweet liberty after a stressful day hanging upside-down.

Mugger braked to a halt alongside the hen, which squawked in alarm and dashed away onto the verge in a heroic bid for freedom. Haroun clambered off the pillion seat and hobbled after her, dragging his right leg behind him.

'You'll never catch her at that speed, cripple.' Mugger jumped off the bike, sprinted past him and dived on top of the errant hen. Haroun ran back to the bike and jumped on.

'Got her!' Mugger raised the speckled hen high into the air, smirking all over his face.

Got her. Haroun squeezed the clutch, stepped on the gear pedal with his left foot and revved the accelerator with his right hand.

'What are you doing?' Mugger's triumph turned quickly to bewilderment and then to fury. 'Don't even *think* about it.'

Haroun bit his lower lip and let out the clutch. The bike moved off. Out of the corner of his eye he saw Mugger drop the hen, saw him running towards the bike.

Clutch, second gear, accelerate. *Don't stall. Don't stall.* Mugger was fast and he was too close for comfort. Clutch, third gear, accelerate. His pursuer reached out to grab the back of the bike and Haroun twisted the accelerator as far as it would go. Mugger clutched at thin air, tripped and sprawled on the road.

Haroun did not hear the curses which Mugger hurled after him in the darkness; riding a motorbike for the first time was more than enough to keep him occupied. He had ridden a moped before but never a big bike with gears. And he had never ridden at night. And he had never ridden to a secret nuclear laboratory. First time for everything.

He took the GPS receiver out of his pocket and glanced down at it. The red dot had passed Tinzar and was heading towards the mine. *So Burayma was right. The yellowcake tribute is going right back where it came from.*

Haroun twisted the accelerator and headed in the direction of the signal, the wind blasting warmly against his eyeballs. *My name is Nuuhu,* he told himself. *I work for Bayt Saïz. I am on my way to the uranium enrichment lab to take photos for my masters. I do not feel fear. Or rather, I do not show it.*

13

As Pleiades rose in the east, desert dwellers all around the Shinn Massif noticed an orange taillight blinking among the stars. Those who strained their ears in the silence of the night detected the hum of a plane's engine.

Three young herders were gathered at the Oursi oasis, warming themselves around a fire while their camels drank.

'Pilgrims on their way to Mecca,' said one, glancing up at the heavens.

'White girls on their way to Agadez,' said another, just to be different.

'Look! It's dropped something,' said a third.

'Where?'

'Over the mountains. *There.*'

'Planes don't drop things.'

'That one did. It was like a tiny seed.'

'Like your brain, you mean?'

'Wait, there are *lots* of them. Little black seeds, like the seeds of the *gurmoohi* tree.'

'Umaru is going bonkers.'

'No, I am not.'

'He's drunk too much camel milk.'

'You're blind, both of you.'

While the boys argued on, eight black parachutes drifted silently down towards the mountains. The GIGN had arrived in Niger.

*

Haroun was homing in on the yellowcake tribute; he was less than two kilometres away, and heading straight for it. The red dot had not moved for over twenty minutes, so perhaps that meant it had arrived at the enrichment laboratory and was being unloaded. Haroun glanced up at the stars and saw the constellation Ali rising in the east. Ali with his belt and tunic and short sword: Ali the warrior. If Ali was rising, it must be almost time for the *rendezvous* with Zabri.

The winking red dot marked a position in the desert less than two kilometres away from the Uranico mining compound. It did not make any sense for there to be a secret laboratory in that location. The landscape was completely flat all the way from the Uranico compound to the Shinn Massif, so in daylight any 'secret' installation there would be visible for miles around. Maybe whoever was carrying the tribute had not yet arrived at the lab; maybe they had simply stopped to camp for the night.

Haroun wished for a moon, but it had not yet risen. Even with his headlights on full beam, he could see only a few metres in front of him. Were it not for the GPS receiver, he would be travelling blind. He glanced down at it for reassurance and what he saw made the hairs stand up on the back of his neck. The yellowcake tribute had completely disappeared off the screen.

Haroun blinked and re-focused his eyes on the screen. There was the flag marking his position, but the red dot marking the tribute was nowhere to be seen. Was the tracker malfunctioning? Or had it been discovered? Did they know Haroun was following a GPS signal? Was he riding into a trap?

Haroun felt like a blind man. He could stumble on the terrorist den at any moment and he would have no warning of it. *Bannde bunndu wanaa fijorde bumdo,* he thought. The mouth of a well is no place for a blind man to play.

My name is Nuuhu, he murmured, trying to calm himself. *I work for Bayt Saïz. Agahan himself has told them to expect me. Agahan has told them to treat me well. I simply have to take a few photos and leave.*

Two bright lights came on in front of Haroun – car headlights shining right in his eyes. He swerved and braked sharply, skidding to a halt in the soft sand. It took a while for his eyes to readjust to the darkness after the harsh glare of the headlights.

'*Salam aleykum,*' said a male voice. Someone was standing over Haroun. He could not see the person but he recognised the guttural tone of a Tuareg.

'*Aleykum asalam,*' said Haroun.

'Turn off your motor and give me the key,' said the Tuareg. French was a romantic language, but this man managed to make it sound hard.

Haroun squinted into the darkness to get an idea of his surroundings. He saw the shape of the pick-up truck nearby but its lights had been turned off again. There were figures moving to and from the truck; some carried loads on their shoulders. *Yellowcake barrels*. Haroun turned off the motor.

'Who are you?' said the Tuareg. 'What are you doing here?'

'My name is Nuuhu,' said Haroun.

'What are you doing here? Who sent you? Who do you work for?'

If you flee from the fennec, thought Haroun, *how will you face the fox?* Ever so slowly he got off the bike and folded his arms across his chest. 'I have travelled far,' he said. 'Bring me some water to quench my thirst.'

The Tuareg spluttered. 'I'll quench *you*, you insolent little—'

'What is your name?' asked Haroun.

'You dare to interrogate me?'

'I have told you my name,' said Haroun, 'and now I am asking yours. I want to be able to tell the Teacher the name of the man who welcomed me.'

His mention of the Teacher did the trick. The man turned to unseen persons behind him and he barked an order in Tamasheq. Haroun got the gist: *Tell Zabri that his guest has arrived.*

'In Algeria,' said Haroun, 'the *imajaghan* are legendary for their hospitality. A weary traveller arriving at an *imajaghan* camp will be given a goblet of water. An invited guest, on the other hand, will be offered tea and dates and—'

'Forgive me,' said the man. 'You must understand that this is no ordinary *imajaghan* camp. Who have you come to see?'

'I do not know,' said Haroun. 'The Teacher referred to him only as Zabri.'

'His name is Foggaret Zabriou ag Issendijel,' said the man. 'Here he is now.'

A skinny arm stretched out of the darkness, shrouded in a wide low-hanging sleeve. Haroun took the proffered hand. He tried to make out the face beyond it but could see only a dim silhouette against the night sky. The bulk of the turban suggested a chief.

'Monsieur ag Issendijel,' said Haroun, wincing at the firmness of the handshake. 'I trust you passed the day in peace?'

'Peace only,' said a cheerful voice. 'Call me Zabri.'

'I am Nuuhu from the House of Saïz,' said Haroun. 'You will forgive me if I ask you the questions?'

'The questions? What questions? Oh, *the* questions. Of course. How quaint.'

Haroun looked down at his hand. Zabri was still holding it in his iron grip.

'Fifty years ago,' said Haroun, 'what did the *imajaghan* desire?'

'A fast white dromedary,' sang Zabriou, 'a red saddle, his sword and a song of love.'

'And today, what does the *imajaghan* desire?'

'A plate of rice, a blanket to cover himself, his sword as a souvenir. So the Teacher told you to ask the questions, did he? How like him. You have no idea, son, how mind-numbingly dull it is to answer those questions every day.'

'Dull but necessary,' smiled Haroun, feeling more confident now. 'You have the product?'

'Of course I do,' said Zabri, squeezing his hand and leading him forward into the darkness. 'Come, young man, you have much to see.'

Zabri did not let go of Haroun's hand as they walked away from the motorbike. Any tighter and the grip would have been painful.

'In the beginning we used torches,' said Zabri, 'but now our men know their way in the dark. It is better this way. Light attracts unwanted attention.'

'Police?' asked Haroun.

'American surveillance planes,' whispered Zabri.

'They spy on the desert?'

Zabri looked at him sharply. '*Bien sûr*,' he said. 'More so now than ever before.' Haroun's mouth went dry. There was lots he should know and didn't. He hoped he could keep up the Bayt Saïz pretence long enough to get into the lab. And, of course, to get out of it.

'This way, please,' said Zabri, letting go of his hand. 'Mind your head.'

In front of Haroun was a small domed hut made of straw. It looked just like a Fulani hut. Zabri was pushing him gently towards the low doorway. *This is no laboratory. It's a trap!*

'What's in there?' said Haroun, trying to keep his voice steady.

'The entrance to the inmost cave,' said Zabri. 'Come on, do you want to take those photos or don't you?'

Haroun did not want to, but he knew he must. If he tried to turn back now, it would be a sure sign of guilt. *Play the game*, he thought, and he ducked into the hut. Zabri followed him in and lit a match, allowing Haroun a brief glimpse of his surroundings.

This was no normal Fulani hut. In the centre of the hut, where the four-poster bed should be, there was a gaping hole in the ground. On one side of the hole there was a metal frame supporting a pulley and on the other side there were rungs leading down. Over in the shadows was a wicker table with a computer on it.

Haroun caught a glimpse of Zabri's face lit from below, the uneven light highlighting creases in the turban and laughter lines around the eyes. Nose and mouth were hidden by folds of rich indigo cloth.

The match burned down to Zabri's fingers and went out. 'Tell me,' he said. 'How long have you been with Bayt Saïz?'

'Long enough.'

'Bien sûr.'

Zabri took hold of Haroun's hand again and led him towards the well. *Bannde bunndu wanaa fijorde bumdo,* thought Haroun.

'Turn round,' said Zabri. 'Crouch down. That's right. Can you feel the first rung? Good. Climb down and I will follow you.'

Far down below Haroun there was a small circle of light. He climbed down towards it, his feet feeling tentatively for each rung.

'Nice climbing, son,' said Zabri.

Haroun did not trust Zabri's laughter lines or his cheerful voice or his relentless hand-holding. Yet on he climbed, rung by rung, down into the fox's lair. *My name is Nuuhu. I work for Bayt Saïz. Agahan has told them to treat me well.*

'Who is the emir of Bayt Saïz these days?' asked Zabri.

'Mustaf Belmustaf du Hoggar.'

'Bien sûr.'

Haroun reached the bottom of the ladder and found himself in a tunnel lit by low-power electric bulbs, just like the galleries in the Uranico mine. Then it hit him: this place must have been *part of* the Uranico mine.

'This tunnel,' said Haroun as Zabri stepped down off the last rung. 'It looks like a mine.'

'It is,' said Zabri. 'But there is no more uranium in these galleries. Uranico dynamited the tunnels two years ago to close them off from the rest of the mine. That's when we moved in. Uranico has no idea we're here.'

Zabri was extraordinarily tall and thin and his

imajaghan robes hung off his frame in loose swathes. He was too tall for the tunnel, so he had to stoop slightly.

'They didn't close it off completely,' said Haroun, pointing up the shaft they had just climbed down.

Zabri nodded. 'That was a ventilation shaft,' he said. 'We widened it to make room for the ladder and the pulley.'

'And the pulley is for hoisting yellowcake up and down?'

'*Exactement.* You see that huge basket on the end of the rope? The one with the barrel in it?'

'Yes.'

'That's the yellowcake basket. It's counter-balanced by weights on the other end. Barrel in basket, the barrel comes down. Take barrel out and the basket goes up.'

A young *imajaghan* came towards them along the tunnel, took the barrel out of the basket and lifted it onto his shoulder. The basket slid upwards into the dark shaft and the porter trudged away down the tunnel, bent beneath his load. *So that's why the GPS signal disappeared*, thought Haroun. *The barrels are being brought underground.*

A stack of iron weights on a rope slid down out of the ventilation shaft and came to rest on the floor of the tunnel. '*Voilà*,' said Zabri, his eyes crinkling at the corners. 'Crude but effective.' He took Haroun's hand and led him along the gallery. They turned left, then right, then left again. They went down a long straight passage with a couple of dozen barrels lined up against the wall. Then left again, then right. Haroun noticed a couple of burst light bulbs in the tunnel ceiling: he could not help it.

'Where in Algeria are you from?' asked Zabri suddenly.

'Tamanrasset.'

'You look to me like a Fulani.'

'My father is Fulani.'

'And your mother?'

'We do not have time for small talk. Where is the SILVA lab?'

'Not far now,' said Zabri. 'What exactly do you want to photograph?'

'Monsieur Belmustaf told me to photograph the enrichment process and the uranium itself. That is all.'

Silence.

'It is a long time since I visited Tamanrasset,' said Zabri. 'Is Al Hadji Haroun still the imam at the *Grande Mosquée* there?'

Haroun jumped at the mention of his own name. *Coincidence, surely.* 'I do not know the imams at the *Grande Mosquée*,' said Haroun quickly. 'I am with the Wahhabists.'

The *imajaghan's* grip on Haroun's hand tightened slightly. Or was he just imagining that?

Before them stood a large metal door. Haroun took the goatskin bag off his shoulder and fumbled for the camera. Zabri put a key in the door and twisted it. 'Welcome to the inmost cave!' he cried, as the door swung open.

Haroun gasped. The room before him was nothing like a cave. It was brilliantly lit and spotlessly clean. The floor and walls and even ceiling were covered with ceramic tiles as white as milk. Three men in white suits and hoods busied themselves around a cylindrical contraption like a fallen tree – except that the trunk of this tree was transparent and filled with red light. Haroun was spellbound by that light. These white-clad sorcerers had captured the setting sun.

'Shouldn't we be wearing radiation suits like theirs?' asked Haroun.

'No need,' said Zabri. 'We won't be in here long. Dr Talata! One moment of your time, *s'il vous plaît*.'

One of the three men came over and greeted them with a nod and a quick handshake. He squinted down at Haroun through the tiny eyeholes in his hood.

Zabri spoke to the hooded man. 'I have brought you a fellow countryman,' he said. 'This is Nuuhu from Tamanrasset.'

Haroun's heart skipped a beat. If this scientist was from Algeria then he would soon realise that Haroun was not. The game was up before it had even begun.

'*Salam aleykum*, Nuuhu,' said Dr Talata. 'What news from the motherland?'

'*Aleykum asalam*,' said Haroun, his heart beating wildly. 'No special news. All is well.'

'If all is well in Algeria, that is special news indeed,' chuckled Dr Talata. 'What brings you to Tinzar?'

'Bayt Saïz sent me to take photos of your work.'

A young *imajaghan* hurried into the lab and whispered something to Zabri – but not quietly enough to avoid Haroun's sensitive ears. *The Teacher wants to talk to you. Something about a helicopter arriving. He says it's urgent.*

Zabri stared at the messenger. 'The Teacher is *here*?'

'He is at the *Bijouterie*. He wants you to call him on the sat-phone.'

'You mean, meet him at chatchatchat?'

'I mean, call him on the sat-phone.'

Zabri looked at Haroun. 'Excuse me,' he said. 'Urgent phonecall at the surface.'

Haroun's heart sank. If Zabri talked with Agahan, he would realise that Agahan had not sent an Algerian boy to take photos. They would know that they had an imposter in their lab. 'I'll come with you,' said Haroun quickly.

'No need,' said Zabri. 'You stay here and take your photos. Talata will show you anything you want to see. I shall be back shortly.' He turned on his heel, ducked through the doorway and swept out of sight. The messenger followed.

Dr Talata turned to Haroun. 'Do you like poetry?' he said.

'No,' said Haroun.

'Pity. Lasers and good poetry are the only beautiful things in this world.'

And cows, thought Haroun, but he did not say so. 'Could I see the lasers?'

'*Inshallah*,' said Dr Talata. He put a hand on

Haroun's shoulder and led him towards the SILVA machine. 'Those are my lab assistants,' he said, pointing. 'Nabil, Gonad, say hello to Nuuhu.'

The white-suited assistants nodded a curt greeting and bent to their work again.

'SILVA has three parts,' said Dr Talata. 'The vaporiser, the laser system and the collector. This here is the vaporiser. In goes yellowcake; out comes uranium gas.'

Haroun took a photo. He found the camera easy to use compared to the GPS receiver. The only hard thing was keeping his hands from shaking when he pointed the camera. *A Fulani does not feel fear*, he told himself. *It is a long way to the surface and a long way back down. Zabri may be some time.*

'The uranium gas is a mixture of two isotopes,' Dr Talata was saying. 'Uranium 235 and Uranium 238. For a bomb we need lots of 235 and as little 238 as possible.'

For a bomb. Haroun shuddered. 'So the aim of SILVA,' he said, 'is to separate the 235 from the 238?'

Dr Talata nodded vigorously. '*Précisement*, dear boy. Look, here are the vacuum tubes which protect the lasers. Beautiful, are they not?'

'You've bottled the sunset,' said Haroun, taking another photo.

Dr Talata chuckled. 'A sunset-coloured laser absorbs Uranium 235 but not Uranium 238. So we pass our uranium gas over the laser and the two isotopes go their separate ways.'

By now Zabri would be at the surface, talking to the Teacher. The photographer is here, Zabri would be saying.

What photographer? the Teacher would reply.

The boy you told me to meet.

I did not tell you to meet any boy.

'These here are the collector plates,' said Dr Talata. 'They collect the Uranium 235 ions and—'

'Where is the final product?' asked Haroun.

Dr Talata's eyes looked hurt. 'The final product is further along,' he said. 'I have a lot to show you before we come to that.'

'You are very kind,' said Haroun, 'but I promised Monsieur ag Issendijel not to interrupt your work for longer than is necessary.'

'Monsieur ag Issendijel works me too hard,' said Dr Talata. 'Guess what time I start work in the—'

'Just show me the uranium, all right?'

The scientist tutted loudly under his hood, and for a moment Haroun thought he was going to refuse. But Talata just shrugged and led Haroun towards a work surface at the far end of the lab. 'By the way,' said Talata as they walked. 'Do you have any news of the border dispute between Algeria and Egypt?'

Haroun clicked his tongue noncommittally. 'No recent news,' he said.

Talata stopped dead. '*Voilà*,' he said, pointing at a tray of smooth whitish coins. 'Weapons-grade uranium. ninety-two per cent Uranium 235. Harbinger of death.'

Haroun raised the camera to his right eye and pressed the shutter. No, that was too blurry. Too much camera shake.

Dr Talata stood at Haroun's elbow, watching him. 'Harbinger of death,' he repeated, rolling the words around his tongue.

Haroun pressed the shutter again, checked the picture and clicked his tongue in disgust. He was known in Uranico for his steady hands, and here they were letting him down.

'There is a line in the Golden Ode of Antar,' whispered Talata, 'that goes like this: *He who dreads the causes of death, they will reach him, even if he ascends the tracts of heaven with a ladder.*'

Haroun took a deep breath and pressed the shutter a third time. This time the photo was crisp: fifteen kg of uranium coins. *If that doesn't bring the French running, nothing will.*

'Silly me,' murmured Talata. 'I've just remembered something. There *is* no border dispute between Algeria and Egypt.'

Haroun put the camera back in his goatskin bag. 'Thank you for your help,' he said.

'In fact,' said Talata, 'there's no border between Algeria and Egypt, is there? Libya gets in the way, as usual.'

Haroun slung the bag over his shoulder, cursing himself for his stupidity. He had studied geography at nomadic school. How could he have let himself be tricked so easily?

'My niece would have known that,' said Talata, 'and she is only four and a half years old.'

Haroun turned and walked quickly towards the door but he could sense Talata following close behind him. 'Your mistake is perfectly forgivable,' said the scientist. 'After all, my niece is Algerian and you are quite clearly NOT!'

Haroun broke into a run. He reached the door a second ahead of Talata and dived through it, slamming it behind him.

An alarm siren began to screech. Haroun wondered as he ran whether Dr Talata or Zabri had set it off. It did not matter much: they were both chasing him now, and so was every other person in this hellhole.

14

Left turn, right turn, straight on, Haroun sprinted towards the exit shaft. Six months of working in a mine had given him a good sense of underground direction, and he had no trouble retracing the route that Zabri had led him. He was already at the long straight stretch, running past the barrels lined up against the wall. From here it should be simple: right, left, right, up the shaft and out into the cool night air.

'Vite, vite!'

'Trouvons-le!'

Haroun stopped and listened. *Zorki*. Whoever his pursuers were, they were between him and the exit. And they were too close for comfort; if he turned right now, he would run smack into them. Yet there was no going back: a reunion with Dr Talata in a dimly-lit tunnel was not something to be desired.

The barrels. Haroun had no choice. He sprinted back to the line of barrels against the wall and lifted the lid of the fourth one. Empty. Haroun jumped inside and pulled the lid back on.

Pullo yidaa ombeede. This barrel was even smaller than the space behind Remy's bookshelves. Haroun had to battle against rising panic. He took deep breaths and thought about the family cows: *Naaye, Baleeri, Mallewe, Wuneewe . . .*

Footsteps echoed through the tunnel, approaching from both sides, running.

'You there! Stop!'

'Who? Me?'

'Ah, Talata, *pardon-moi*. Where is that boy I brought to see you?'

'He ran away,' said Talata. 'Whoever you said he is, he isn't.'

'I know,' said Zabri. 'Where did he run to?'

'He came this way. Haven't you seen him?'

'No.'

Eere, Saaye, Terkaaye . . .

'Well then,' said Talata. 'If I'm chasing him and you haven't seen him, logic would suggest that he is sitting in one of these barrels.'

'Let's see if you're right. I'll start here and you start at that end.'

Amare.

'He's not in this one.'

Jamalle.

'Or this one.'

Oole.

'Or this one.'

Huroy.

'*Le-voilà!* Here he is.'

Haroun looked up into Zabri's eyes and wished he could disappear. Of all the ways he could have lost tonight's game, this was surely the most humiliating.

'*Salam aleykum, mon petit éspion,*' said Zabri. 'What are you doing in there?'

'Hiding,' said Haroun.

A white hood with tiny eyeholes appeared alongside Zabri. 'Strictly speaking,' said Dr Talata, 'that's what you *were* doing. Before we found you.'

A third head appeared, turbanned in brilliant white. Between the dark twinkling eyes there was a bump the size of a cola nut. Haroun groaned. It was Burayma's uncle.

'*Salam aleykum,*' said Abdullai baa Samba. 'This is not very original, is it, son? Hiding in a barrel.'

'It's been done before,' said Zabri.

'*Treasure Island,*' said Talata.

'*Ali Baba and the Forty Thieves,*' said Abdullai.

The three men peered into the barrel and shook their heads at him.

'What happens now?' said Haroun.

'We help you out of that barrel and ask you a few questions,' said Abdullai baa Samba. 'And then, *inshallah,* Dr Talata will kill you.'

*

Lieutenant Henri Lupin was getting worried. None of his men had said anything – they were too professional for that – but he could tell what they were thinking. *Still no word from Agent H. He is in trouble. He needs us.*

The squad had regrouped in a small crater in the foothills of the Shinn Massif. They had hidden their parachutes in a deep crevice. They had checked and double-checked their desert camouflage, radios, bullet-proof vests, night-vision goggles, gasmasks and ammunition. They had eaten grey army-issue biscuits out of unmarked foil packets. They had studied the Uranico compound through monocular night scopes. They had synchronised their watches. And now they sat in grim silence, waiting for the call.

Lupin looked down at the GPS receiver in his hand. Remy had been wise to give Agent H the Satboots. As well as the bug under the tongue of the right boot, there was a GPS device concealed in the sole of the left boot which emitted a pulse every 60 seconds. Even in the plane on the way from Satory, Lupin had been able to follow Agent H's progress across the desert, all the way to a point a couple of kilometres west of the Uranico mine.

But there the signal had suddenly disappeared. The only explanation was that Agent H had gone underground. He was cut off. He could not be tracked by GPS and nor could he send his photos. Perhaps his life was in danger.

The motto of the GIGN popped into Lupin's head: *Servitas Vitae. Save lives.* Yet what could he do? *Le Commandant* had given him clear orders that very afternoon: if Agent H did not make contact by sunrise, he was to abort the mission and return to France. The situation was delicate, *le Commandant* had said. It would be diplomatic suicide for French Special Forces to intervene without concrete proof of uranium enrichment.

Henri Lupin cradled his submachine gun in his lap and gazed up at Orion, which was now directly over his crater. Orion the hunter. Orion with his belt and dagger and bow and arrow. *Get out of there, Agent H. Get out of there and make the call.*

*

'Lasers and good poetry,' said Dr Talata, 'are the two most beautiful things in the world. If I were in your shoes, I would not want to be killed with a dagger or a gun. I would want to be killed with a good poem or a laser.'

Haroun and the scientist were alone in the SILVA laboratory. Abdullai baa Samba and Zabri were at the surface waiting for the helicopter to arrive. As for Nabil and Gonad, Dr Talata had told them to go and get some sleep, and they had been only too happy to oblige. They had taken off their radiation suits and hung them up on the far wall of the lab, and then, with one last pitying glance at Haroun, they had hurried out.

'I have never heard of a man being killed with a good poem, or even with a bad one,' said Talata. 'Have you?'

Haroun shook his head and strained against the cords which bound him – neck, hands and feet – to the chair he was sitting on. No good. He was as helpless as a hobbled camel.

'I have heard of a man being killed with a laser,

though,' said Talata. 'As it happens, my predecessor in this job was killed with a laser. It was a terrible accident. He slipped and fell onto the dye pump laser.'

'Who told you that?' said Haroun.

'Monsieur ag Issendijel.'

'And you believed him?'

'Of course,' said Talata. 'Monsieur ag Issendijel is an honourable man. If he were not, I would not work for him. You, on the other hand, have been deceiving me all night.'

'Sometimes deceit is necessary,' said Haroun.

'Deceit is despicable,' said Dr Talata. He flicked a switch on the wall and the vacuum tube emptied instantly of its red glow. 'Do you know what the wandering desert Arabs in the time of Zuhair used to do? When they met in the desert, they would present the blunt ends of their spears to each other if they intended peace and the pointed ends if they intended violence. You always knew where you were with a wandering desert Arab.'

Slowly and deliberately, Dr Talata unscrewed the metal cap on the end of the tube. Then he swung the apparatus around on its axis so that it was aiming directly at Haroun.

'This here,' said Talata, 'is the pointed end of the spear, so to speak.'

'Why do you do it?' said Haroun, trying to keep the fear out of his voice. 'Why do you live down here making instruments of death?'

Talata shrugged. 'The poet Zuhair said that

Death is like the blundering of a blind camel. He whom he meets he kills, and he whom he misses, lives and will become old. There is no logic in Death, no reasoning with him. I do what I do.'

'But what do you get from it?'

'Lasers and poetry. I work with beauty and I am rewarded with beauty. Have you ever heard of the Golden Odes?'

'Stop, oh my friend,' said Haroun. *'Let us pause to weep over my beloved Unaizah. Here was her tent on the edge of the sandy desert between Dakhool and Howmal.'*

Dr Talata raised a hand and pulled back his hood. He had greying hair and pale blue eyes and he looked very tired. Haroun was startled to see that his blue eyes were brimming with tears.

'The traces of her encampment are not wholly obliterated even now,' quoted Talata softly. *'For when the South wind blows the sand over them the North wind sweeps it away.'*

'The Golden Ode of Imru-Ul-Quais,' said Haroun. 'It was one of six poems stolen from the Jeddah Museum a few days ago.'

'It's beautiful,' said Talata, wiping away the tears with the sleeve of his lab coat. 'Even hearing a few lines of Imru-Ul-Quais makes me weep.'

'Me too,' said Haroun. 'It is probably the most beautiful poem ever written.'

Even as the words left his mouth, Haroun realised that he had overdone it. Dr Talata blinked and shook his head from side to side as if trying to break a spell.

'I asked you earlier whether you liked poetry,' said Talata, 'and you said no. Now you say that Imru-Ul-Quais is so beautiful it makes you weep.'

'That's why I don't like poetry,' said Haroun quickly. 'It makes me weep so much that I lose track of where my cows are, and they end up wandering off and getting—'

'Silence!' shouted Dr Talata. 'I refuse to wade any longer in the swamp of your untruths.'

The scientist strode to the wall and reached for the laser's ON switch. 'Prepare,' he cried, 'for a head-on collision with the Blundering Camel of Death!'

He flicked the switch. The SILVA apparatus hummed into life and a beam of red light shot out of the mouth of the vacuum tube, hitting Haroun on the forehead.

'SILVA lasers are very low powered,' said Talata. 'For the first two minutes your head will feel pleasantly warm. Then you may experience some discomfort. It will take at least five minutes for the laser to melt the skin, and another ten to pierce your skull.'

Haroun tried to shift in his chair but the ropes which bound him were too tight. So this was it. He was going to die.

'*Adieu,*' said Dr Talata, walking to the door. 'I will come back in half an hour and clean up.'

The scientist paused with his hand on the door handle and a strange look came over his face. 'Six,' he said.

'What?' said Haroun.

'You said that six poems were stolen from the Jeddah Museum a few days ago. You meant to say seven.'

Haroun cast his mind back to his conversation with Remy. The heat on his forehead was making it hard to think. 'Six,' he said. 'I'm sure of it. Six poems were stolen.'

'One, two, three, four, five, six, *seven*.' Talata beat the air with his forefinger. 'The Seven Golden Odes. Why would they be called the *Seven* Golden Odes, if there were not seven of them?'

'There *were* seven of them,' said Haroun. 'But only six were stolen. The seventh one must still be hanging in the Jeddah Museum.'

The scientist began to pace up and down the length of the glowing vacuum tube. 'Six Golden Odes,' he muttered. 'That's not right. I asked for all seven. They promised me all seven. Six is worse than none!' He whirled round to face Haroun, his face contorted with rage. 'You are lying again!' he shouted. 'Deceit is DESPICABLE, do you hear me?'

'It's the truth,' said Haroun quietly. 'Ask Monsieur ag Issendijel.'

A long silence followed. Haroun closed his eyes. The heat on his head was almost unbearable.

'All right, I shall,' said Dr Talata. 'I shall ask him straight away. I shall put the Blundering Camel on pause until we get this sorted out.'

He hurried to the wall and flicked the OFF switch. The laser shut down.

'Thanks,' said Haroun. 'Be careful what you say to Issendijel. If you upset him you might end up having a terrible accident.'

'Like what?' said Talata, heading for the door.

'Like falling onto a dye pump laser, said Haroun.

Dr Talata left the laboratory and locked the door behind him. He was greatly agitated as he hurried along the galleries of the mine. The thought that one of the Golden Odes might have evaded his grasp made him feel physically sick.

He arrived at the ventilation shaft and climbed the ladder into the straw hut which masked the opening.

Talata ducked through the doorway, out into the cool night air. It was the first time since his arrival here that he had been out of the mine, and the feeling of space and freedom made him feel better straight away.

Zabri was standing by the entrance to the hut, gazing up at the full moon, which had just started to rise. The scientist's sudden appearance made him jump. 'What are you doing here?' snapped Zabri. 'I thought I told you never to come to the surface.'

'I felt sick,' said Talata. 'I needed fresh air.'

Zabri softened. '*Bien sûr*,' he said. 'I would have dealt with the boy myself,' he added, 'but the Teacher told me to wait for this helicopter.'

'*Pas de problème*,' said Dr Talata. 'Where's baa Samba?'

'Call of nature.'

'I see. You said you would give me another ode, if I terminated the boy.'

'And so I will.'

'Which one?'

'The Golden Ode of Tarafa.'

'Aah, dear Tarafa.' The scientist's eyes misted over. 'Tarafa, the rebellious boy whose verse cost him his life. Don't give me Tarafa yet.'

'Okay, I'll give you Labid.'

'No. I would prefer the Golden Ode of Al-Harith.'

Zabri frowned. 'Who?'

'Al-Harith the leper chief, whose battle songs were so thrilling they made people's eyes bulge.'

In the silence that followed, Dr Talata could have sworn he heard Zabri's teeth grinding.

'Monsieur ag Issendijel,' said Talata, 'you do *have* the Golden Ode of Al-Harith, do you not?'

'Of course,' snapped Zabri. 'But I decide the order in which you get the poems, not you.'

'Why is that, Foggaret?' Talata took a step nearer to the tall, thin *imajaghan*. 'What does it matter to you whether you give me Tarafa or Labid or Al-Harith? *Unless, of course, one of them is not in your possession.*'

'We will talk about this later,' said Zabri. 'I can hear the helicopter coming.'

It was true. The sound was quiet but getting steadily louder.

Talata took another step closer to the *imajaghan*, and stood on tiptoe so that he could whisper in his ear. 'The Golden Ode of Antar,' he said, 'has a line which goes like this: *When I am not ill-treated, I am gentle to associate with.*'

'We will talk about this later,' repeated Zabri, but his voice was not as steady as before. 'Go back to your laboratory and wait for us there.'

*

Henri Lupin's eyes ached. For the last hour he had been watching the straw hut through his monocular night scope and there was still no sign of Agent H. The only people he had seen were grown men. Right now there were two such men standing by the door of the hut, deep in conversation, but even with the night scope set to x6 magnification Lupin could not make out their faces clearly.

A helicopter was coming. By the sound of the rotor blades he judged it was a Cougar X40. Yes, there it was, flying high to the south, heading straight towards them. Had someone found out about the GIGN presence here? Was this a welcoming committee?

His men had also seen the threat. They dived for cover behind crags of rock and waited for their commander's instructions. Lupin interlaced his fingers and lifted them to his right shoulder. *Prepare the surface-to-air rocket launcher.*

'Do not fire until I give the order,' said Lupin.

The squad's second-in-command peered into his night scope. 'That bird is not military spec,' he said.

'Are you sure, Pierre?'

'Yes. No guns.'

He was right. Lupin watched with mounting

relief as the helicopter banked left and circled above the straw hut to the east. Whoever this was, they were obviously not here to eliminate GIGN soldiers. They were here on business.

The helicopter landed fifty metres east of the hut. Two smartly dressed men jumped down and were greeted warmly by the tall Tuareg.

'What do you think?' said Pierre, studying the visitors through his monocular. 'Middle East?'

'Hard to tell at this distance,' said Lupin. 'Central Asia, I would say.'

'What about the pilot?'

'Niger.'

'No, I mean what about her? Cute, isn't she?'

'I have no opinion on that,' said the lieutenant dryly.

The visitors disappeared into the hut with their host. A Tuareg in white robes and turban stayed outside; he wandered over to the helicopter and began to talk to the pilot.

Lupin re-focused his monocular and did a quick scan of the open desert behind the hut. *What was that?* Someone was approaching the hut on foot. It was a boy. And he was accompanied by a small cow.

Lupin looked down at his GPS receiver, but it was still blank. *If that boy is not Agent H, who is it?*

*

Haroun tried to free himself but the cords which bound him were too strong. A key turned in the lock and Dr Talata entered the laboratory.

'Wherever I go,' said the scientist, 'I smell the stench of dishonour.'

'Does Zabri have the seventh Golden Ode?' asked Haroun.

'He does not.' Dr Talata leaned back against the SILVA vacuum tubes and rubbed his eyes hard like an overtired child. Then he approached Haroun and untied the cords which bound him. 'The Blundering Camel has had laser eye surgery,' he said. 'You will not be meeting him today.'

'Thank you, doctor.'

Dr Talata went to a safe in the wall and took out a battered briefcase and a goatskin bag. He threw the bag to Haroun. 'Farewell,' he said. 'I am leaving this mire of untruth.'

'What will you do? Where will you go?'

'I shall look for the Golden Odes of Tarafa and Labid,' said Dr Talata. 'After that, I shall fill a leather water-bag and enter the desert's empty wastes.'

'Good luck,' said Haroun.

Talata looked at him. 'Do not let anyone see you on your way out. Monsieur ag Issendijel seems to think you are dead.'

'I will need a disguise.'

The scientist waved his hand towards the radiation suits hanging on the wall. 'Take your pick,' he said.

'*Salam aleykum.*'

'*Aleykum asalam.*'

Talata left the laboratory and the door clicked shut behind him.

Haroun jumped up from the chair and ran over to the radiation suits. He chose the smaller of the two – it was still too big for him, but at least it would hide his face and his herding clothes. As he climbed into the suit he happened to glance down at the exit tube of the SILVA apparatus. He gasped. Talata had left the tray of enriched uranium coins right there on the work surface.

Haroun put on the radiation gloves, scooped the uranium into his goatskin bag, slung the bag around his neck and zipped up the radiation suit over it. Then he pulled the floppy hood over his head so that the holes lined up with his eyes. The uranium felt heavy around his neck and he knew how dangerous it was to carry it so close to his body. He must get to the surface as quickly as possible and send those photos to Henri Lupin.

The tunnel leading away from the laboratory was deserted, but Haroun resisted the impulse to run. He was a lab assistant now. *Lab assistants do not run; they walk.* Left, right, straight on past the barrels, right, left. Haroun arrived at the bottom of the exit shaft and peered up into the darkness. A foot came into view, and another. Someone was coming and there was no time to run. *Please don't be Zabri.*

The person who stepped down off the ladder was not Zabri, and he did not look like a Tuareg. He was a squat man with a moustache and grey eyes. There was something interesting about the shape of his face and eyes. Haroun and the stranger looked at each other and the man nodded at him almost shyly. Haroun put his palms together and returned the silent greeting.

A second man stepped off the ladder. He was older than the first but had the same colour skin, not Arab but not quite *tuubaaku* either. *'Bonjour,'* said the newcomer and his hesitant pronunciation showed he was not a French-speaker.

Haroun bowed slightly and stepped forward to go up the ladder, but there was yet another person coming down. *Please don't be Zabri.*

It was Zabri. He stepped down onto the floor of the tunnel, wiped his hands on his robe and beamed at his guests. 'Nice climbing, friends,' he said, and his guests grinned back at him uncomprehendingly.

Zabri suddenly became aware of Haroun standing there. 'Ah, Nabil, there you are,' he said.

Haroun nodded vigorously. He could be Nabil if Zabri wanted him to be. At this moment anything was better than being Haroun.

'Where is Dr Talata?' asked Zabri. Haroun pointed vaguely down the tunnel which led to the laboratory.

'Good,' said Zabri. 'Come with me, friends. You have much to see.'

The three men began to move off down the tunnel, and Haroun was just about to shin up the ladder when Zabri turned and addressed him again. 'Nabil,' he said. 'If you're taking a break, could you give your suit to Mister Kasparon here? I have told him there is no danger, but he is very anxious about radiation.'

Haroun froze. He could not unzip the suit without Zabri recognising his clothes and his goatskin bag. And he certainly could not take off his hood.

'Nabil?' said Zabri. 'Are you all right? Did you hear what I said?' Then his eye fell on Haroun's boots. 'You!' he roared.

The roar was quite enough to unfreeze Haroun. He jumped onto the third rung of the ladder and scampered upwards as fast as his hands and feet would carry him. The rungs vibrated as the giant *imajaghan* jumped onto the ladder below him.

'Son of a cockroach!' bellowed Zabri. 'I'm going to tear you apart!'

15

Haroun scrambled upwards, taking the rungs two at a time. His life depended on him getting to the surface before Zabri, but the uranium was heavy around his neck, weighing him down with every step.

'It's a long way up, is it not?' said Zabri, and his voice was too close for comfort. 'I do this climb at least eight times a day, so I should know.'

Haroun's foot slipped off a rung. He hung by his arms, casting around frantically to regain his footing. *There.* He was on his way again, but his whole body was trembling. *He who dreads the causes of death, they will reach him, even if he ascends the tracts of heaven with a ladder.*

'What's the matter?' said Zabri. 'Did you nearly fall off?'

Haroun felt a hand on his left boot and he kicked down viciously to make it let go. A wave of nausea swept over him; there was no way he could beat this *imajaghan* in a race to the surface.

'One of the advantages of being two metres

tall,' said Zabri, 'is that I can take rungs three at a time. Long arms, that's the secret.'

Time to get tough, thought Haroun. He stopped climbing and unzipped his suit. 'I've got the uranium!' he shouted. 'If you climb one more rung, I'll drop it.'

Silence.

'I'm not bluffing!' shouted Haroun. 'Each one of these coins contains enough neutrons to blow us all to Agadez!'

Silence, and then an explosion of mirth from below. It started as a guffaw and turned into a deep belly laugh, its echoes rebounding back and forth off the walls of the shaft until it sounded to Haroun like a whole caravan of *imajaghan* was laughing at him.

'Wait until I tell this to Dr Talata,' cried Zabri. 'You think those coins are little nuclear bombs, do you? Drop one down the shaft and it explodes when it hits the bottom? You're in the wrong job, son. What are you, a cattle herder?'

Blood rushed to Haroun's cheeks. He turned back round to face the ladder and started climbing again.

'I'll tell you what would happen if you dropped one of those coins,' called Zabri, climbing up after him. 'Our Teraqi guests down there would pocket it and ask you for the rest. Ha ha ha!'

'Go suck a laser!' shouted Haroun.

'Haroun, is that you?'

This time the voice had not come from below.

It had come from above. And it had spoken Fulani. *Hamma. What was Hamma doing here? How had he found this place without GPS?*

There was no time for questions. 'I'm being chased,' yelled Haroun. He felt ashamed to be asking his brother for help. What could Hamma do anyway? Hamma was up there and Haroun was down here and Zabri was clawing at his boots.

There was a commotion up above and then Hamma's voice came again: 'Jump across onto the rope!'

The rope? How would that help? The rope would simply carry him back down to the bottom.

'Haroun! The rope!'

From the darkness above him there came a loud whirring and a moo. Haroun recognised that voice – *Terkaaye!* Only then did he realise what his brother had done. *Hamma, you brute. You've put my favourite cow into the yellowcake basket.*

There was no time for recriminations. Haroun launched himself through the air towards the rope on the other side of the shaft. He caught it with both hands and hung on tight. The rope did not take him down; it took him up, and fast. As he sped towards the surface Haroun passed the large basket and its occupant plummeting in the opposite direction. The astonished moos of Terkaaye faded into the darkness below.

The pulley was approaching fast, and Haroun

knew he would have to time his jump to perfection. If he jumped too early he would fall back down into the shaft. If he jumped too late he would mash his hands in the pulley mechanism.

Haroun stretched out his left hand so that it brushed against the wall of the shaft. The moment he felt the wall come to an end, he let go of the rope completely. A pair of strong hands caught him by the wrists and hauled him over onto solid ground.

'*Salam aleykum*, brother,' said Hamma. 'Nice suit.'

'*You zorkin skink-wit!*' yelled Haroun, pulling off his hood. 'Do you realise what you've done?'

'I've pushed Terkaaye down a well,' said Hamma. 'Don't thank me now, thank me later. Do you have the keys to that motorbike outside?'

'I do, but what about Uncle Abdullai?'

'He's busy chatting up a pretty pilot,' said Hamma. 'I got past him with Terkaaye so I should be able to get past him with you, don't you think?'

The boys ducked out of the hut into the moist night air and sprinted towards the motorbike. Haroun jumped on, turned the key in the ignition and kicked the starter. His brother hopped on the back and they were off.

Haroun shifted into second gear, then third. Off to the right, the helicopter stood motionless in the moonlight.

'Uncle Abdullai has seen us,' said Hamma. 'He's shouting something. He's shaking his fist. He's heading for the pick-up truck.'

Haroun bit his lip and leaned forward. The sand was too deep for fourth gear so he stayed in third and twisted the accelerator as far as it would go. He had the headlights on full beam but did not really need them any more. The moon was full tonight and it had risen high into the night sky.

'Someone has just come out of the hut,' said Hamma. '*Zorki*, he's gigantic!'

'His name is Foggaret Zabriou ag Issendijel,' said Haroun. 'He doesn't like me.'

'I know how he feels,' said Hamma. 'I follow your tracks all the way from *Cyber Alpha*, dodge baa Samba, push a pretty cow down a well, save your life and what do I get for my trouble? I get called a skink-wit.'

Haroun unzipped his suit with his left hand and took the bag off his shoulder. 'Shut up and take this,' he said. 'I want you to send some photos to Henri Lupin via the sat-phone.'

Hamma took the bag. 'Is that all? I thought for a moment there you were going to ask me to do something difficult.'

Haroun leaned left so that the bike was heading straight for the Shinn Massif. Once the truck got going it would not be easy for a bike to outrun it, but they would have a better chance in the foothills of Shinn. With any luck there would be passages there too narrow for Abdullai to get the truck through.

'What's Zabri doing?' asked Haroun. 'Did he get in the truck with Abdullai?'

'No,' said Hamma.

'Phew.'

'He got in the helicopter.'

'*Zorki*.'

Haroun adjusted his wing mirror. Sure enough, the blades of the helicopter were rotating, slowly at first, then faster and faster. He adjusted the mirror again and saw the Toyota careering towards them in hot pursuit.

'Two more men have come out of the hut,' said Hamma. 'They are running towards the helicopter. They are getting in.'

'They're Teraqis,' said Haroun. 'I expect they want their uranium back.'

'Could you go a bit faster?' said Hamma, shifting his weight nervously on the back of the bike.

'Could you talk a bit less?' said Haroun. 'Have you sent those photos?'

'No,' said Hamma. 'I haven't opened the bag yet.'

'Open it.'

'Okay.'

'Take out the camera.'

'There are lots of little coins in here,' said Hamma.

'Don't touch them. Have you got the camera?'

'Yes.'

'Have you got the phone?'

'Yes.'

'There's a cable in there somewhere.'

'Got it.'

'Connect one end to the camera and the other end to the phone.'

'Okay.'

Haroun looked in his wing mirror and saw the helicopter lift off the ground, nose downwards. It straightened up and hung in the air a moment, then the nose went down again and it powered forward.

'I've connected them,' said Hamma. 'I think.'

'Right. Turn them both on.'

'How?'

'Never mind, just give it all to me.'

Hamma reached forward and plonked the camera and phone in Haroun's lap.

'I will need my hands free!' shouted Haroun. The helicopter blades were thrashing close behind them already. 'Take hold of this handle and keep it twisted towards you as far as you can.'

Hamma put his chin on Haroun's shoulder and reached forward to take hold of the accelerator. Haroun glanced in his wing mirror again. The truck's headlights were horribly close but the sound of its engine was drowned by the rotor blades of the helicopter.

Haroun switched on the camera and the satellite phone.

TRANSFER PICTURES?
OK

The helicopter was overhead now, flying low a little to the left of the bike. Haroun glanced up and saw one of the Teraqis leaning out, the one with the moustache and the grey eyes. He did not look shy any more; he looked angry. And he was holding an assault rifle.

'Lean left!' shouted Haroun, as bullets rained down onto the sand. The bike swerved underneath the helicopter and out the other side.

Haroun's thumbs skittered on the keypad of the sat phone.

VOILA LES PHOTOS.
VENEZ VITE!

The helicopter banked left and came in for the attack. Haroun's button-pressing became frantic as he scrolled through menu after menu. *What had Remy said about attaching photos to a message?*

At last!

ATTACH PICTURES?
YES
CHOOSE PICTURES TO ATTACH
ALL

A volley of bullets raked the sand and some of them ricocheted off the body of the bike close to the petrol tank. Haroun stepped on the footbrake and the pick-up truck rammed into them from behind, smashing the back mudguard and making the bike wobble dangerously. Haroun put a foot down to regain balance. A bone snapped.

FIND NAME IN ADDRESS BOOK.
LUPIN

They accelerated again. The pain in Haroun's foot was excruciating; he was so dizzy he could hardly read the sat-phone display. *A Fulani man is governed by pulaaku,* he told himself. *Whatever happens to him, he retains his dignity, his reserve. A Fulani man feels no pain.*

SEND MESSAGE?
YES
SENDING . . .

The sand was shallower now, and stonier. The black-topped mountains of the Shinn Massif loomed before them.

Hamma was muttering in Haroun's ear. 'I feel sick,' he said. 'It's the uranium, I know it is. I'm being irradiated back here.'

'Look on the bright side,' said Haroun. 'From now on, you won't need a torch for night-herding.'

SENDING . . .

Out of the corner of his eye Haroun could see the truck drawing alongside them. Abdullai baa Samba grinned broadly and waved at them.

'See that lump on his forehead?' said Hamma. 'I did that.'

Haroun looked up; the helicopter was directly above them and coming down. *That woman is going to land her helicopter right on our heads.*

SENDING . . .

'Take these,' said Haroun, passing the phone and the camera to Hamma. 'Now that we're out of the sand, let's see how fast this thing can go.'

Haroun took over the controls from his brother, engaged fourth gear and twisted the accelerator to the max. The wind blew hard against his cheeks and the pursuing truck slid backwards out of his field of view.

'OH, LA VACHE!' cried Hamma behind him. 'We're flying!'

There was a rocky slope ahead, leading up into the foothills of the Shinn mountains. Haroun shifted down a gear and leaned low over the handlebars as the bike shot up the hill. The thick tyres skimmed over the smooth rock and flung up fragments of gravel on both sides.

'What does the display on the phone say?' shouted Haroun.

'Message sent,' read Hamma. 'Is that good?'

Haroun forgot the pain in his foot for a brief

moment and let out a yawp of triumph. The photos had gone through.

The motorbike sputtered and began to lose speed.

'Switch to the reserve petrol tank!' shouted Hamma.

Haroun bent down to look at the two-way switch next to his left knee. 'That *was* the reserve tank,' he said.

'*Zorki*, brother,' said Hamma. 'Our milkcow just dried up.'

The slope levelled out onto a smooth table of rock nestled in the foothills of Shinn. The bike juddered halfway across the plateau and stalled.

The helicopter had overtaken them and was hovering low over the moonlit plateau. The thrashing of its rotor blades echoed off the rocky crags on both sides. It lowered gently down onto the flat rock in front of the motorbike. Haroun saw the loose end of Zabri's turban flapping in the downdraft of the rotor blades.

He turned and squinted at the headlights of the Toyota as it laboured up the hill and rolled to a halt about twenty metres behind them. The door opened and out stepped Abdullai baa Samba, assault rifle under his arm. *That's what the imajaghan desires today*, thought Haroun. *A plate of rice, a blanket to cover himself and a smuggled Kalashnikov.*

'*Salam aleykum!*' cried Zabri, jumping down from the helicopter. 'You ride well, Nuuhu. Mustaf Belmustaf would be proud of you, if you existed. Hand over the uranium.'

Haroun looked at his brother and shrugged. 'Give it to them,' he said.

Hamma took the goatskin bag off his shoulder and threw it to Zabri. As the Tuareg bent to pick it up, a small grey fruit rolled between his feet.

The fruit was the size of a guava but knobbly like breadfruit. Judging by the *imajaghan's* reaction, it was not one of his favourites. He leapt away from it and dived to the ground. Haroun saw a blinding flash of light and heard a bang so loud that it seemed to have gone off inside his own head.

There followed a long silence. Haroun felt the cool hard granite against his cheek and against the palms of his hands. He opened his eyes and rolled over, his whole body stiff and heavy like on the second day of a malaria fever.

The smoke cleared. Zabri, Abdullai and the two Teraqis were lying face-down on the plateau. Their hands were on their heads and they were surrounded by men in loose sand-coloured robes.

Haroun shook his head slowly from side to side. Someone was crouching beside him, speaking French.

'Agent H? Comment ça va? Tu m'entends?'

It took several minutes for Haroun's sight and hearing to begin to feel normal again. He was given water from a heavy flask. He was offered biscuits but he had no appetite. His broken foot was sending shooting pains all the way up to his hip and back.

'That straw hut down there,' the man was saying. 'Is that an entry-point to the lab?'

'Where is Hamma?' asked Haroun.

'He's fine. Is the straw hut an entry-point?'

'Yes. There is a vertical shaft leading to the galleries.'

'Elevator or rungs?'

'Rungs.'

'How many?'

'I don't know.'

'Fifty rungs? One hundred?'

'I don't know. A lot.'

'Are there guards at the bottom of the shaft?'

'Yes. No.'

'How many men in the mine?'

'Five. Maybe more.'

'How do you get to the lab?'

'Right, left, right, straight on, right, left.'

'The door of the lab – what is it made of?'

The questions continued, on and on and on. Haroun's head ached. His foot was agony. He wanted to go home to his cows.

When the questioning was over, Henri Lupin assigned one of his men to look after Agent H and another to guard the prisoners. Then Lupin went across the plateau to the abandoned Toyota, got in the passenger seat and pulled the visor of his helmet down. Pierre, his second-in-command, sat in the driver's seat and three other soldiers got in the back. Their faces were pale with anxiety and determination.

'*Allons y,*' said Henri Lupin.

Throats tightened. Adrenaline began to flow. The drive to the straw hut took seven and a half minutes, but it seemed much longer. It had been this way on all of Lupin's previous missions. The approach to a hostile target always dragged. He checked the barrel of his Manurhin revolver and replaced it in its holster. The truck stopped by the straw hut and they jumped out.

As soon as they were inside the hut, time sped up. They were clipping carabenas to their belt buckles. They were throwing lightweight ropes into the shaft. They were sliding down. They were in the tunnel, Henstal submachine guns at the ready.

First things first. The soldiers made their way along the tunnel, following the overhead power lines back to their source, a petrol-powered generator at the end of one of the galleries.

'*Night,*' said Lupin, and his men donned their IL T21 night-vision goggles. The lieutenant drew his *Manurhin* revolver and fired three rounds into the petrol tank of the generator. It exploded in a massive fireball and all the lights in the mine went out.

'*Objective one complete,*' said Lupin. '*Generator disabled.*'

The squad returned to the entry shaft and then headed for the laboratory. Right, left, right, straight on. The spotlights on their submachine guns danced along the walls and floor of the galleries.

As he neared the next bend, Lupin heard

footsteps. They were getting closer. Someone was coming round the corner towards them.

'*Hostile ahead!*' he shouted. He dropped to one knee and raised his Henstal P90.

A black muzzle came into view, but it was not the muzzle of a gun.

'Subject not hostile,' said Pierre. 'Subject bovine.'

They left the little grey cow to wander the tunnels. When this was all over someone else could figure out how to get it up to the surface.

'*Hostiles ahead!*'

This time it was true. Four men with Kalashnikovs were blundering towards them in the dark. Lupin threw a stun grenade and followed it with a controlled burst of fire from the P90. The shots passed low over the rebels' heads, ninety bullets in six seconds, and the rebels sprawled on the ground, unhurt but terrified.

'Pierre, stay here and cover them,' said the lieutenant. 'The rest of you, come with me.'

The soldiers moved on, bunching together at every corner, stun grenades and P90s at the ready.

'*Hostile ahead!*'

The target wore a white suit but it looked pale green through the T21 goggles. He carried a briefcase in one hand and a pale green canister in the other.

'*Biological!*' shouted Lupin and he switched on the laser aim-point of his P90. He had seen harmless-looking canisters like this before. He had seen what they could do to people.

The man in the white suit looked down with interest at the five tiny red laser-points dancing over his heart. He gave a peculiar laugh and raised his hands into the air.

'He's going to throw it!'

Three shots rang out and the canister fell to the ground.

'Gas masks!' An ecstasy of fumbling. The soldiers donned their masks in seconds.

No gas came. The lieutenant ran forward and picked up the canister. 'What have I done?' he murmured.

It was not a canister, it was a tightly rolled scroll. Lupin unfurled it and saw that it was two sheets of linen, each covered in beautiful gold-writ Arabic calligraphy.

'Tarafa.' The dying man's voice was little more than a whisper. 'He too was killed because of his verse. I suppose there are worse ways to go.'

16

'How's your foot feeling?'

'Fine.'

'Fulani fine, or fine fine?'

'Fulani fine.'

'Bad luck.'

Haroun and Hamma were sitting on a large flat rock not far from the helicopter. They had blankets around their shoulders and were sipping coffee from large enamel mugs.

'Do you think Terkaaye is okay?' asked Hamma for the third time.

'No,' said Haroun. 'I think you killed her.'

A soldier was sitting nearby, watching the straw hut through an odd-shaped tube. His radio crackled into life.

'This is Lupin,' said a voice over the radio. 'I am at the surface.'

'I can see you, Lieutenant,' said the soldier. 'How was it down there?'

'Objectives achieved. SILVA laboratory secure and all hostiles neutralised.'

'Ask him if he found our cow,' said Haroun.

'Lieutenant, Agent H is asking whether you saw a cow down there.'

'Tell Agent H that Agent Cow is alive and mooing. Pierre and the others are hoisting her up as we speak.'

Relief flooded Haroun's body and he passed out.

*

When Haroun came to, he was in Tinzar hospital and his foot was set in plaster. Hamma and Remy were sitting on the end of his bed.

'Remy!' cried Haroun. 'They let you go!'

'Yes,' said Remy. 'Thanks to Blaise Soda.'

'Soda?' Haroun frowned. 'It was Soda who had you locked up in the first place!'

'Yes. But when I told him that the rebels had SILVA, he was rattled. He visited the Teacher at the *Bijouterie* to find out whether I was telling the truth.'

'And?'

'The Teacher did not deny it. In fact, he offered Soda money to keep quiet.'

'Five million African francs,' said Hamma, popping a cola nut into his mouth.

'He must wish now that he had never made that offer,' said Remy. 'He will probably spend the rest of his life in prison.'

'What about Abdullai baa Samba?'

'Definitely looking at a life sentence. I still have that tape from the acid vat, remember? He confessed to the murder of Claude Gerard.'

'Good,' said Haroun.

'There is one thing, though,' continued Remy. 'The trials will be held in secret. The truth about the yellowcake tribute must never be known.'

'Why not?' cried Haroun. 'Why shouldn't it be known?'

'Because Uranico would close down and the economy of Niger would collapse. Millions of people would suddenly be even poorer than they already are.'

'*Ko nyolli fuu luuban*,' said Haroun. 'Whatever rots, stinks. You can't cover up something this big.'

'You'd be surprised what can be covered up,' smiled Remy. 'Here in the Sahara the sand blows over everything.'

Haroun sat up in bed. 'Are you telling me that Soda will carry on as mine director as if nothing has happened?'

'Blaise Soda is not a friendly man,' said Remy, 'but he is certainly a clever one. He reckoned that by paying the tribute he was saving innocent lives. As things turned out, he was right.'

'No thanks to him,' said Haroun. 'What would have happened if it weren't for Baleeri walking in front of that lorry and Terkaaye throwing herself down that mine-shaft?'

'Indeed,' said Hamma, spitting out a mouthful of cola nut juice. 'And Eere cracking that code and Naaye planting those bugs. See you later, brother, I hope the delirium doesn't last all day.'

'Where are you going?'

'Herding,' said Hamma. 'Our four-legged heroes are hungry.'

Hamma left the room and shut the door gently behind him.

Remy turned to Haroun. 'That job I offered you at CAL, our Communications Analysis Laboratory,' he said. 'How about it? We could use a good pair of ears like yours.'

'No,' said Haroun firmly. 'Spying is for violinists, shoe-shiners and medicine pedlars.'

'And librarians,' added Remy.

'Exactly,' said Haroun. 'But not for me. I'll stick to my cows!'

$$| \equiv \bigcirc \qquad \bullet \equiv \qquad \} \odot \equiv +$$

$$ \mathsf{I}\mathsf{=}\bigcirc \quad \bullet\mathsf{=} \quad \mathsf{\}}\odot\mathsf{=}\mathsf{+} $$

● http://www.chatchatchat.com/room101/javaapplet.js